FOR THE LOVE OF MURDER

A miscarriage of justice

Alan C Bruce

Disclaimer

I invite you to enjoy this entirely fictional story direct from my imagination; therefore, all characters, places and events have been made up to tell this story to entertain the reader. Any resemblance to persons living or past is purely coincidental along with events and conversations. It is my sincerest hope you enjoy my work.

To my wife, Dennie,
Twenty-seven years of marriage, one daughter, several pets (not including Goldfish), eleven houses, two countries, and I have lost count of how many secular jobs; In all of this, you have been my one constant.
Thank you.

I will always love you.

Contents

This is the mark of a really admirable man: steadfastness in the face of trouble – Ludwig van Beethoven

Chapter One

Last train to Edinburgh

I t was night; the clouds were heavy with the promise of rain.
Tom and Jane stood on the platform edge holding each other's hand; she was the greatest love of his life. If only he could somehow find a way to tell Jane how much he feels about her, then perhaps she might decide to stay. Time was running out for them both; she would leave for Scotland and almost certainly be out of his life forever. He needed to say something; if he did not say something, then soon it would be too late.

The train pulled into the station, steam billowing out of the sides like a horse ready to bolt on a cold frosty morning. Tom gazed at her longingly, his throat dry, his muscles unable to move him closer to steal a kiss. Desperately he hoped that she would change her mind and stay with him as he held onto her hand a few moments longer.

"Last train to Edinburgh!" Tom looked away from Jane to see a rather portly station master calling out with a loud commanding voice. They both knew it would not be long before he called once more.

"Time to board!"

Desperately trying to cling onto the last few moments, he held her hand just a little tighter; she looked back at him, gazing into his deep brown eyes, hoping he would tell her to stay. As a lady, Jane knew that she could never tell him how she felt first. She wanted to be with him, but it had to be his choice; he would have to say that he loved her first.

Suddenly, the train's boiler let out a head of steam, signalling to all it was now time to leave. To on-lookers, this could have seemed mawkish to those watching the scene play out. However, for Tom and Jane, it was intense and real.

"Time to leave!"

The station master once again called and blew his whistle; he was trying to give them as much time as possible; he had a schedule to keep to; that was more important to him. Jane turned her head and looked towards the carriage door, which was still open, calling her to her destiny. As she began to walk away, still holding on to his hand. Their fingers slipped slowly and longingly through each other's fingers until the moment they drifted apart forever. Knowing it was now too late, Jane reluctantly boarded the train and closed the door behind her. She pulled the window down, desperately hoping to hear if Tom would muster up the courage to say how he felt about her. Jane stood there waiting in hope, in vain; the train began to move slowly at first until it gathered speed, leaving Tom all alone on the platform.

Tom could only stand there watching as the train gathered pace whilst it moved slowly and progressively further away from him until it eventually disappeared into the night. It might have seemed like a scene from a movie to anyone else watching. Almost as if some way, this was not happening to them both. He stood there for what must have seemed an eternity to any on-lookers, looking down the track as if somehow, he could have made the train reverse towards him. Then looking down to the platform floor, he knew it was all over.

The station master looked at Tom with a warm smile and said, "never mind, I'm sure you will see her again." Tom, however, was not so sure; he certainly believed he had lost Jane out of his life forever. In that moment of realisation, he turned around and walked out of the station. Crossing the street to the late-night café, and took refuge inside as the rain began to fall harder.

Once inside the café, he took a table by the window. He just sat there saying nothing, hardly even acknowledging the waitress as she spoke to him, "what you need; is a drop of something strong and a nice cup of tea. Brandy suit you?"

Tom looked up at her; he gave a half-hearted smile, which was all he could manage under the circumstances and said, "thank you, that will be perfect."

Glowering out of the window into the night, Tom could hardly believe she was gone, and perhaps with her, his only chance at real happiness.

What a fool I've been! he thought to himself; *if only I had been stronger, I could have stopped her from leaving, but now it was all too late.*

Tom gulped down the brandy, scarcely even touching the hot, strong tea that became colder by the moment.

And I'm supposed to be the man, strong, confident! He scorned himself. *Out of all the things I've seen and done, I should be better than this; and stronger! How could I have been such a fool,* his negative thoughts almost taking over completely?

On the other hand, Jane calmly took her seat on the train. She had a small compartment for the journey. Jane made herself comfortable, took a white handkerchief from her bag, and gently dabbed her eyes. Jane hoped her makeup had not smudged, especially her mascara. Jane did not want to appear as if she had been crying or arrive looking like a panda from the world-famous London zoo.

What is so wrong with me? she asked herself.

Jane felt all alone. *Why could he not tell me how he felt?* Jane knew she had fallen deeply in love with him, but for her to tell Tom was not the done thing. She was sure he felt the same way she did about him, believing even to the last minute that Tom might say to her directly or give a clue to what he was thinking.

The train pulled further from the station and away from Tom. Jane resolved in her heart, knowing it would take all her strength. Jane knew it would take every ounce of resilience that she could muster to do this. Somehow she would put this, including how she felt about Tom, behind her and move on with her life.

Tom sat in the cafe deep in thought, berating himself in his mind, till what had seemed an eternity had passed, barely noticing what was happening around him.

"I'm sorry, I need to lock up now. We're closing."

"Sorry, I didn't realise the time."

"That's ok, finish your tea first. I can wait a few moments more; It's not like I have anyone to go home to."

Tom wasn't sure if the waitress was being sarcastic or not. She didn't seem the type to be. The conversation was enough to bring him back into reality. After Tom gulped down his tea, He stood, thanked the waitress for her hospitality, put on his hat and coat and left the cafe, not forgetting a tip.

"Good bye, Sir. Stay safe."

Chapter Two

The passage of time

Ten years passed; Tom had barely given another thought to that rainy night in November 1945. When he and Jane said goodbye, they knew it would be the last time they saw each other again.

Tom was sitting at his dining table. One hand holding his daily newspaper, the other rummaging between a half-eaten slice of toast and his morning cup of tea. Tom found himself drawn to an article entitled, "Another miscarriage of justice!" The news article asked the question no one else wanted to. "Has the killer struck again?"

"There have been two suspicious deaths in Edinburgh; two girls of similar age were found dead in a quiet country lane. Both of the girls, have not been named. It's also believed that both girls' bodies had been positioned to resemble a past case from ten years ago. The case in question was regarding a man called Paul Barry; he had been tried, convicted and sentenced to hang for his crimes."

Tom had been deep in thought; the sound of the dog barking brought him back to the present moment. Barking had become his usual morning ritual when the post came. This always excited Emily, who was only six years old and found copying highly amusing.

As he stood and casually walked over to the door, his heart began to thump uncontrollably. He looked down at the mat and saw a letter postmarked Edinburgh and the unmistaken handwriting of Jane, his long-lost love.

Thoughts of that time unexpectedly came crashing into his mind, thoughts he almost found hard to control.

What if he had been more courageous and told Jane how he felt about her? Maybe, even telling her he loved her, just what might life have been like for him now?

He placed the letter into his jacket pocket, not daring to open it now, preferring a more private moment. His mind is racing. *What could Jane want after all this time? Why now?* Perhaps more importantly, *what would his loyal wife Mary have to say?*

He tried to put his thoughts on the subject to one side. Almost instinctively, he expected this day to be an important one. He was not sure why. He had hoped it would be positive. However, with the sickening feeling in his stomach, coupled with the news article and now a letter from Jane. Tom knew beyond a doubt that today would not be easy.

Tom sat at the table, closed his eyes, and breathed in through his nose. After holding his breath for a fraction of time, he exhaled to calm himself down and recapture his composure. Could he have the case from 10 years ago so wholly wrong and played a defining role in the conviction and hanging of an innocent man? The thought was almost too overwhelming for him.

"Darling, is everything alright?" Mary asked.

"Yes!" he replied rather quickly. Tom hoped not to alarm Mary. News of this magnitude could be devastating. Who knows how she might react; after all, she might be married to a man who had made an appalling mistake. How would she cope?

Looking up at her, he smiled as she handed him his lunch for the day. "Thank you; I don't know where I'd be without you, looking after my every need; you are my savour."

Mary smiled at him and said in a kind and gentle voice, "you looked like you needed saving all those years ago when you walked into my café on that dreadful night." The couple giggled to themselves.

Noticing the time, Tom quickly kissed Mary and Emily goodbye; whilst putting on his hat and coat and rushing out the door. The journey to work had seemed uneventful, except it seemed to be over quicker than he might have wanted. As Tom walked to his office, he felt nervous; more than butterflies in his stomach; this was akin to a panic attack, although not completely. Tom had never suffered this way before and wasn't sure how to handle these feelings. He hoped no one else had made a similar connection and may start pointing the finger.

His only thoughts were, *how could he even begin to put this right? Where could he start? And how would his young family cope with what he had done?*

Tom made it to his office; after closing his door and pulling the blinds, Tom sat at his desk with his head in his hands. Panic had not quite taken hold of him, but he knew it would not take much more to push him over the edge.

There was a knock on the door. Janice, the old lady from the canteen, who always had a soft spot for him, brought him his usual cup of tea and a biscuit on the side. "Cheer up duck! it might never appen, mi dear."

His composure soon came back, albeit quite briefly, "thank you, you always know how to cheer me with a decent cup of tea. How are you?"

"Yeh, I'm good my lovely, not so for the old man though, he's avin a bit grief wiv is hip, but we soldier on, no sense in complaining."

"Very true, but you give him my best wishes and thanks again for the tea and chat."

"That's what I'm here for, mi dear," she said as she hurried out of the office to serve others with her unmistakable east-end charm and a cuppa.

It was at that point and, quite alarmingly, the phone rang. Tom's heart sank; he thought he knew what was coming next. Cautiously, he answered, "Hello, inspector Richards speaking." He paused, hoping not to give himself away.

"Hello, Tom. Now, look here! I'm sure you've heard about the death of these two girls in Edinburgh, and I'm sure I don't have to tell you how serious this could be for us all, especially you. My counterpart in Scotland has requested your presence immediately, and I intend to make-sure he gets all the help he can. So, I want you on the overnight train to Edinburgh, no if no buts. Do I make myself clear?"

"Yes, sir!" Tom said, hoping to ease the situation. Tom sat back at his desk; for the second time that day, he drew another large breath.

He had barely enough time to think when a second knock on the door came, this time from a young P.C

"Excuse me, sir," the young constable paused briefly, "I've been asked by upstairs to drive you back home to collect your things and then on to the train station."

Tom just looked at him; he was now quite sure the young P.C and perhaps, more importantly, everyone else in the station also knew what was going on. Tom chose to reply courteously and say, "thank you."

On the journey back to his home, Tom kept silent, not wishing to add more fuel to the drama now unfolding with him directly in the middle of it. Silently looking out the window, his thoughts returned to the letter he had hidden inside his jacket, "why now?" He kept asking himself. With all that was now going on, how could he think about reading the letter?

As a detective, curiosity, which is the mark of a great detective, did creep up on him, prodding him to open the letter. Still, he chose to keep it for another time.

Mary saw the car pull up outside and at once felt disturbed in the pit of her stomach. She knew that something was wrong, very wrong. Mary had been baking all morning after Emily had gone to school. She so often did. Baking sometimes reminded her of her years working in the café making homemade cakes and bringing them in for sale. She also loved to do baking for her family made her feel needed. It also gave her home a warm, comforting smell for her family to come home.

Mary heard the keys turn in the lock.

"Daring, is that you? You're home early!"

Mary didn't get a reply. Fearing the worst, she ran to greet Tom at the front door. Mary could see something was wrong. Tom looked pale from worry. Trying not to look worried, she greeted him with a tender kiss. Not like the ones in the movies, but just enough to reassure him that everything, no matter how big or small, everything would be all right. Mary was sure nothing could ever change how she felt about him.

"What is it? Why are you home so early?" So many questions; Mary caught herself thinking of more to ask but tried hard to reign herself back to let him speak.

"I've...well, I think we should go and sit down in the living room first; it might be easier to hear what I have to say." Tom led the way with Mary closely behind him.

"What is it, darling, your worrying me?" Mary could sense the hesitation and hear the tremble in his voice, which made her feel more uneasy.

"Before we met," Tom said cautiously, hoping to alleviate any fear before continuing. "I worked on a double murder; we believe there might have been more victims; we just never found evidence. We did, however, eventually make an arrest. The man was tried, convicted, sentenced, and hanged for his crime. It was in all the newspapers at the time." Mary just looked at him silently, almost too afraid to interrupt him. "Well, it's like this; the man convicted had an evil side to him. His two victims, both females, had both been sexually assaulted, their eyes removed. Then their bodies were moved, placed in an ally and a small white handkerchief placed over each of their faces." Tom paused, realising that the graphic detail might upset his wife further. "I'm sorry, you didn't need to hear all that." Mary silently took his hand. She could see this was hard for him and let him continue. "Some of these details of the crimes we never released, now ten years on there have been two suspicious deaths in Scotland with the same details."

Mary looked on in almost complete disbelief as she realised the full import of his words; she tried hard not to say anything and to let Tom continue. "I know everyone is thinking the same, including me. What if I got it wrong? What if we tried and convicted the wrong man? I'm not sure I could live with that burden on my mind." His eyes welled up as he tried hard not to lose the battle between dignity and sorrow.

Mary listened in silence, trying hard to take in everything he said. All she felt she could do was sit, holding his hand in support. Then in the true British style, inspiration hit her, "what you need," she said, "is something strong along with a nice cup of tea." Tom recalled the last time Mary said that to him, and just like last time, all he could manage was a half-hearted smile and to say, "thank you."

Mary left him alone on the sofa to make the tea; from the kitchen, she could see him deep in his thoughts, contemplating every scenario. It wasn't long before she returned with two cups of tea, one for the constable who brought him home and the other for Tom.

He looked up to receive his tea. As he did this, he noticed out the corner of his eye members of the press circling outside. To him, they looked like vultures waiting for the dying moments, ready to pick at the juicy flesh. The press, he thought, was always prepared to weave any piece of misinformation or half-truth into a story. The intent would be that they could sensationalise it to increase its circulation. He knew a few of the faces, although not by name; he knew enough to know they were not always, in the pursuit of any truth, just a great story for their readers.

Tom had always kept his distance from the press, knowing that they often muddied the waters in any investigation. And when they did this, it made any hope of conviction that much harder; this would now be much harder; he was now at the centre of any story they wrote. *Should he bring them in close?* He thought to himself, should he still try and keep one step ahead of them?

Tom decided the best thing to do was treat the investigation in Scotland as new and different. After all, the original jury in the trial, including him, were convinced they had the right man.

After taking two or three sips of tea, Tom went to his small writing desk, unlocked the drawer and pulled out his original case notes. Packing them into his briefcase, Tom moved upstairs to pack for his trip.

Mary followed him up, sat on the bed and said, "I believe you always do the right thing." Tom could not be so sure; his mind flashed an image of himself hiding the unopened letter from Jane in his inside jacket pocket. Trying very hard to put a brave face on things, Tom began to pack warm clothes into another case, along with a picture of Mary and Emily. Mary went downstairs to the kitchen.

Thirty minutes later, Tom appeared at the bottom of the stairs, his suitcase in one hand and his briefcase in the other. "All set, sir?" the young P.C asked as he came in through the front door. "I've arranged for another car to pick you up from the back of the house to avoid the press outside, sir."

"Excellent thinking, constable. You'll go far thinking like that." With that, Tom passed along the passageway into the kitchen. Mary was standing with a small thermos flask, sandwiches, and a large slice of fruit cake she had been baking earlier. With a large, overconfident smile, she kissed him goodbye, not knowing when he would be back. "Give Emily a kiss from me!" Tom said as he headed out the kitchen door.

"I love you. Call me when you get settled!" Mary called. Tom walked up the garden path and out into the ally, where an unmarked car was waiting to take him to the station and a future that may change his life forever.

Chapter Three

The train journey

S tanding alone on the platform. Tom recalled how he had stood here once before. This time, it was different; he was going away, not knowing what to expect at the other end. The train was going to be forty-five minutes late, according to the station master. So looking around, he noticed the café still open where once he had sat, berating himself for not having the strength to tell someone how much he loved them.

Tom decided out of curiosity to walk over and look inside for old time's sake. After all, why should he not; it was where he met his wife, Mary, albeit sometime after. Tom allowed himself the indulgence to think back to that night and Jane. Although they had only known each other briefly. Tom knew that something more powerful than could be explained had happened, a spark between them that had caused a burning flame stronger than he could have ever imagined. *What would have happened if he dared to tell her exactly how he felt*? He thought.

"Hello, Tom, how are you?" came a voice from across the other side of the room. It was Maggie, Mary's friend and one-time co-worker.

"Hello Maggie, I can't believe you are still here!"

"I know I'm part of the furniture now. I don't think I could leave now even if someone came in from the train station opposite and whisked me off my feet." She giggled, "after all, isn't that what happened with you and Mary?"

"Yes, something like that, although it was some time after my first visit."

"Is there anything I can do for you?"

"No, I'm just killing time waiting for my train and thought I would pop my head through the door to say hello, you know. that sort of thing."

"Do you want a cup of tea; on the house?"

"No, I'm ok, thank you. I've not long had one, but thank you all the same."

Tom had not wanted to stay too long. So clutching his bags, Tom said goodbye and wandered back over to the platform. The wait for the train did not seem so bad now. He was happier having visited his memories, some good and some not.

The train soon arrived; he climbed aboard, took his seat, and tried to settle himself for the long journey ahead. *It was going to be a long night*, he thought to himself. *I should try and get some sleep.*

This would prove to be more difficult than he had ever thought. Tom closed his eyes and rested his head against the carriage door. His thoughts soon returned to the original case. His mind examined every aspect in detail, searching for clues he may have missed. This all mixed with thoughts and emotions of what might happen if he met Jane again in Edinburgh.

His thoughts blasted with the image of Paul Barry, the murderer. Tom could barely clear his mind. The creaking sound and the sudden thump of the gallows as the noose around Barry's neck tightened. The events gave way to an eery silence except for the creaking sound of the rope as it swung back and forth. He could almost taste the unmistakable musty smell from the rope that hung from the gallows. The foreboding look of the gallows sent shivers down his spine as the body released its hold on life. Tom had watched intently as Barry's feet scrambled in a hopeless attempt to find the ground. Memories that will never leave him or his dreams.

Tom awoke in a startle! Almost calling out in fear, just as the guard arrived to tell him that it would only be one hour before they would reach Edinburgh Station. Tom looked at his watch; the time was 5:30 in the morning, could he really of been asleep all that time. "Thank you," Tom said as he tried to adjust himself and make himself more presentable. His thoughts returned to the small provisions his wife had made him earlier. As he opened his food, a small white piece of folded paper fell onto his lap. It was a note from Mary, he opened it and read it twice, it said: "*I love you xxx.*"

The thought of Mary's note to him made the tea and sandwiches taste better. Knowing that back home, someone loved and cared for him. Tom was sure that this would be all he would need to get him through the next few days.

Then almost without warning, his mind jolted him and reminded him of the letter he had received earlier that day from Jane. "What should I do? Should I read it?" he felt almost reprehensible with feelings of guilt even keeping the letter, let alone reading it. He placed his hand inside his jacket pocket to check if the letter was still in place, safe and secure. At this moment, he realised he had changed his jacket earlier in the afternoon and had forgotten to swap the letter into his current blazer. His heart sank with a sick feeling. He knew the letter was now at home in his original jacket; that's placed across the back of a chair just ready for Mary to find and perhaps read.

There was nothing Tom could do or say without arousing suspicion in Mary, for all he knew; he would have to face the consequences when he got back home. *Could his life now get any worse*? He thought to himself. The only time he did find the courage to tell someone how much he loved them; now he was still going to lose her over something trivial? Tom hadn't even read the letter. After all these years, he was sure Jane had not declared her undying love and passion in a letter to him, could she?

The train was only moments away from arriving at the station, trepidation followed by anxiety at what was to come building to an almost impossible wall to climb over. The train now came to a stop. The carriages shuddered to signal the journey's end and a new one about to begin.

Tom opened the carriage door and instantly met with a cold rush of air, "this was enough to wake you up if you needed such a thing," he thought to himself. Looking across the platform, Tom could see another young P.C standing warming his hands, trying to overcome the cold, lonely wait for the train to arrive.

Stepping off the train onto the icy platform, Tom asked, "Are you here for me?"

"Are you inspector Richards?"

"Yes, I'm inspector Richards; what's your name, constable?" Tom asked in a bid to be a little formal yet trying hard not to sound like he was here to teach them a thing or two.

"My name is Robert, but everyone calls me Rabi, like the poet."

"Thank you for meeting me. I hope you didn't have too much of a wait out in this freezing weather."

"No, not really, anyway we're used to it," unlike you Sassenachs, Rabi thought, but not daring to say for fear of retribution.

Tom smiled and shook the constable's hand, "none the less Rabi, it's still good of you."

"Thank you, sir. I have a car waiting to take you straight to the station."

Rabi led Tom to the waiting car; took him straight to the station, not even stopping to find some digs for the next night.

The apprehension Tom felt was considerably high. Whatever may lay ahead of him, he would have to face bravely regardless of where the road took him or the pressures facing him if he had been wrong all these years. This was made worse by having little to no sleep and going directly to the station. However, he was a professional man; he knew his job well and how to do it properly.

Chapter Four

Journeys end

There was not much conversation in the car on the way to the police station, which probably suited everyone well. Tom had no idea how much Rabi knew of the two suspicious deaths in Scotland or how much he knew of the original case back in London in 1945.

At first, Tom thought it was better to keep his cards close to his chest. *At least until he could work out who his allies were. After all, this was a new city to him, and the only person he knew was Jane; that was a lifetime ago.*

The car stopped outside the station on Duddingston road; standing there before him was a building smaller than he had expected for such a large city, although it still looked formidable to him, for more than one reason.

Rabi held the door open, "this way, sir, sign in at the desk and then I will show you to the canteen. You should be able to get a decent cup of tea there."

"Thank you, Rabi, that is just what I need."

Tom decided that he would act with confidence in the hope of not feeling intimidated by his surroundings and being somewhere alien to him. He walked in through the front door to the main desk, signed the visitor logbook, and was escorted straight to the canteen.

"Here you go, sir, help yourself to tea or coffee."

"Thank you, Rabi."

"No problems, I've got to sort a couple of things out, but I will be back as soon as possible. Don't get into any trouble!"

At least Rabi seemed to have a sense of humour. Tom thought as he looked around, trying to take it all in.

He walked towards a counter and noticed a large pot with a sign saying, caution hot! He lifted the lid and peered inside. *Hmm!* one thing was immediately apparent, it wasn't hot and added to this, it did not look tasty.

He stood there trying to convince himself that he should at the very least try it; someone, he was sure, had made some effort to make it.

"You can try it if you like. It's probably been there since yesterday morning, and who knows what it could do to a southerner like you?"

Tom quickly turned around and there in front of him was a face he recognised.

"It's you!" Tom said with his voice slightly more pitched, "they've got you up here too!"

"I could not believe it when I heard an inspector Richards was coming from London. I had to come and see for myself."

"So, what brings you to Edinburgh, Bob?"

I've been working here for about eight years. I married a Scott's girl and got a transfer after our last case together. Do you remember it, Tom?"

"Yes, you did a good job taking the lead as a detective. I knew you had it in you."

"Your too kind, Tom. It was only you're training on that awful murder case two years earlier; if you want any help on this one, you only have to ask; I'm happy to lend a hand."

"A friendly face should be enough for now. Have you heard anything about the death of these two girls?"

"Yeah, it's gruesome! You know, there are a lot of similarities to our old case? I guess that's why you're here. We didn't get it wrong back then, did we?"

"I hope not, Bob. We shall have to see where the evidence takes us."

Tom did not want to commit himself at this stage without seeing the case notes, and if they had got it wrong, he was not going to say so without being very sure. He could not afford another mistake.

"It's good to see you again, Bob."

"And you, Tom. Don't forget, if you need anything, let me know."

"I will bear that in mind, thanks."

There was a pause in the conversation, "Anyway, I've got to go. I'm working on a fraud case, got a briefing in ten minutes, can't be late."

Bob said, remembering how Tom had reinforced the idea of punctuality so many times in the old days.

Tom looked at him, smiled and said, "thanks for popping by to say hello. Maybe we can catch up a bit more later."

"That sounds great. If you ask for me at the desk, the Sergeant will know where I am,"

Bob said as he also disappeared, leaving him alone with his thoughts.

Tom again felt all alone looking around the grey, empty room. It all seemed strangely familiar, even though he knew he had never been here before. *The room was grey in colour and grey in personality.* Tom thought to himself. There was a familiar sound of the lights as they hummed in a low tone. It was the same in just about every station he had worked.

Tom sat down, and after opening his briefcase, he pulled out his case notes and once again searched through them, trying to familiarise himself with every detail.

"I'm back, sir, was everything all right? did you get yourself a cup of tea?"

"No, I looked around a bit. Then sat down here to read my notes."

Tom chose not to tell Rabi that he had met an old friend at this stage.

"Well, sir, if you're ok, I need you to follow me. The boss wants to meet you."

They walked through a long corridor, and at the far end was a door marked chief inspector.

Rabi knocked on the door and paused briefly before walking in. Standing before them was a larger-than-life man, easily six feet plus. He had balding ginger hair and an accent as broad as his shoulders. Tom looked up at him, trying to stand taller and thrust his hand out to shake the chief inspector by the hand. The chief just looked at him and said, "I don't have time for your southern niceties; I have murderer to catch!"

Tom was dismayed by the abrupt approach. He had, however, come across it many times in his career and tried to push it to one side.

"I've already seen the official case notes. I had them sent to me yesterday. I assume you have brought your notes!"

"Yes, sir, I have them with me now."

The chief inspector just stared at Tom, "well, hand them over! Don't just stand there!"

Tom did not appreciate the tone of voice from his new superior; however, he chose not to say anything at this time. he preferred to keep his powder dry, as the old expression goes.

"Here you go, Sir,"

Tom knew his notes would contain his thoughts on his old case and Paul Barry. He also knew it was the best practice to hand everything over to the chief as it may help everyone involved.

"When can I take a look at the case notes for the two girls, sir?" Tom asked. The chief inspector ignored Tom's request, not even acknowledging he was still in the room. At the same time, he carefully looked through everything Tom had written.

Rabi took his queue, turned to Tom, and said, "come on, I'll show you what we have so far." Tom followed Rabi out of the room without any acknowledgement from the chief. Once out of earshot, Rabi said to Tom, "don't mind the chief; he is like that with everyone. What he lacks in social skills he makes up in honesty and commitment."

Tom felt a little reassured enough to ask Rabi a question. "What should we call the chief inspector; he didn't tell me his name?" Rabi just laughed and said, "If he wanted us to call him by his name, he would have told us; most of us just call him Chief; he seems to respond to that, and I probably shouldn't tell you what the rest us call him, we don't want it getting out."

Tom at once felt more at ease having that little bit of knowledge. It seemed to settle his nerves a bit, although he knew from experience that he should not let his guard down just yet.

Rabi had led Tom into a small room. There were no windows, just a fluorescent light suspended from the ceiling, which flickered for several moments before eventually lighting up. This made this room feel more like a large cupboard than an office.

The walls were nicotine yellow in colour with metal racking that followed the wall most of the way around. Tom at once recognised the setup. It was all too familiar; they had a room like it back home. It is where they stored the evidence they were accumulating before any conviction they might obtain.

Rabi told Tom that he could use this room to look at the evidence they had so far. "It is all here." He said. Tom was familiar with this type of room and responded by asking to see the crime scene photographs for the first victim only. Rabi pulled them from a box marked Sarah V1 and handed them to Tom, knowing that this simple act now marked the beginning of something bigger than he had ever seen.

Tom said nothing. All the while looking intently at the few pictures of Sarah that now clearly made him think of his original case. A sick feeling came bubbling up from the pit of his stomach; the similarities between these victims and his were obvious. Tom thought to himself as he continued searching for any clues that might say otherwise.

Tom spent the next few hours without saying a word, scrutinising everything written about Sarah. This included the circumstances Sarah was found. Tom looked closely at every detail in the photos and tried to recall every detail he could from his old case. Ten years is a long time to perfectly remember the details, even for him. Tom had not even noticed that Rabi had long since left the room. He had also forgotten about Mary, his wife waiting at home for a call to let her know he was all right.

Tom sank himself deeper into his thoughts. Detective work had always been about thinking. He was trying to piece together clues that would otherwise seem unimportant to everyone else, matching them with evidence found at the scene to form a larger picture. This picture would tell everyone without a doubt who this murderer was.

Time passed Tom by quickly. Before he realised it, he had forgotten about his feelings and that of everyone else around him, including that he was in a strange city, miles from home.

It was early evening when Rabi arrived back at the office.

"How are you doing, Tom?"

"Not so bad, thanks, Rabi. I see you have brought Bob back with you!"

"Yes, we have a plan for you to consider."

Bob stepped forward and said, "I have had a word with my wife and told her you are here from London, and she agrees that you can't spend your first night here on your own. We have decided that you must come to our home for dinner tonight. Rabi has kindly agreed to take you to a B&B and then on to mine. Isn't that right, Rabi?"

"Yes, Sir, I don't mind, but you will have to make your own way home afterwards, as I will need my beauty sleep."

"Well, it would seem you both have it all sorted out; how could I possibly say no now."

Chapter Five

Cuckoo!

Tom and Rabi soon arrived outside the B&B, which for Tom was to be home for the unforeseeable future. It seemed unremarkable on the outside, a neatly trimmed hedge with a black iron gate breaking the neat line beaconing you to the blue door.

Before Tom had the chance to knock on the door, it opened. "Hello, my name is Hannah, Han for short if you like, and this is my husband, Steve; come in, come in out of the cold."

Hannah, the landlady, was full of enthusiasm and perhaps a little on the quirky side; not quite eccentric, but she had an unusual way about her.

"This is my husband, Steve. Say hello, Steve."

Steve smiled and not much more; Steve was more reserved, a man Tom thought he could identify with, preferring to watch and observe.

"You must be the detective we have heard about from London!" Steve said confidently. Tom just smiled politely. Tom was slightly overwhelmed by Han's enthusiasm. Han, as she preferred, seemed rather excited at the idea of a London detective staying at her B&B.

She had long dark hair, brown eyes, lightly freckled skin, and a slim frame. On the other hand, Steve was slightly portlier with blond/grey hair and was more of a thinker than a speaker. It was clear he ran the B&B but was happy to let Han think otherwise. Rab collected the bags from the car. He put them in the hallway and told Tom he would be back a 7 pm sharp to take him to Bob's house for dinner.

Hannah quickly said that the doors were always locked at 11:30 pm without exception "you can't be too careful nowadays." She said with a little twinkle in her eye. Rabi saw this as his opportunity to leave, bidding them all goodbye until 7 pm.

Tom stood silently, taking in the eclectic mix of décor and ornaments, which seemed to clutter every inch of the hallway and beyond. Without warning and alarmingly, the sound of a cuckoo clock chimed the hour, reminding everyone it was six o'clock.

"Isn't it wonderful?" Han blurted out, "it was a gift from a couple who stayed here every year; they gave it specially to say thank you for their time here. Can you guess where they were from?"

Tom wanted to say, "Swiss cottage, London?" Although he thought better of it and decided to reply, "Switzerland?" He was now quite tired, and being polite became a little bit harder, and besides, they might not get the humour.

Steve, the landlady's husband, took Tom's bags up to his room and beaconed Tom to follow, "I'll show you to your room, it has a nice view out to Arthur's seat, and it's quite peaceful."

Tom was led to the very top of the stairs to what looked like an attic room; after opening the door, he stepped inside. The room was pleasant enough and had everything he would need for a good night's sleep.

"Each room has its key; we serve breakfast from 7 am till 8 am, no earlier, no later; if you want a cup of tea, just let us know there's always one in the pot."

"Is there a telephone?

"I, just on the corner of the street only a few yards away,"

Tom had remembered his promise to Mary and did not want to leave it any longer before calling. He thanked Steve, smiled, and immediately proceeded down the stairs and out of the door to the phone box on the corner to call his dear wife.

The phone box was still its usual bright red colour, and to his amazement, it took English pennies. Tom started to feel quite at home with this familiarity. However, he was a little nervous at hearing his wife's disapproving voice at not phoning sooner. His concerns melted almost instantly at the warm sound of Mary's voice.

"Hello, it's me, Tom."

"Hello Darling," Mary said instantly, "how is Scotland?"

Mary knew Tom would feel guilty over not phoning sooner. She was also very aware of the difficulties Tom could be facing and decided not to take him to task over it. As Tom spoke, a few small tears welled in her eyes. Mary just wanted to be there with him as a family and everything back the way it was. She knew that was impossible right now and had realised that the best thing she could do was to be supportive. Mary composed herself and told Tom how Emily had drawn him a picture at school and wanted to post it to her Daddy in Scotland so that he would not forget her.

Tom just paused, catching his breath. He told Mary the new address for the station and the B&B that would become home for him for some considerable time. Tom described the cuckoo clock and the strange eclectic house. He also told Mary about the landlord, a husband a wife team who seemed larger than life. They thought this was a great adventure for them, having a London detective staying with them to help solve a double murder.

It wasn't long before the conversation paused, each listening to the other, their soft breathing saying more than words ever could. The silence now reminded Tom of back in 1945 at that train station with Jane, although this time it was different; it was him that had gone away and had left Mary all alone. After a few moments of silence, Tom spoke up and asked, "Has there been anything of interest in the post?"

"A small amount, although they look like bills, nothing interesting."

Tom replied in a casual voice, "oh! Ok, I'll sort them out when I'm back; by the way, I've left my jacket on the back of the chair. Sorry should have hung it up."

"That's all right; Emily and I decided we should keep it there until you return. We can then pretend you are still with us here. Emily has put the photo of you on the table from the mantelpiece and asks you questions pretending you answer her.

Tom took some comfort in that, although he was still more concerned about the letter from Jane. His heart pounded for a moment as he quickly thought about all the possibilities and scene that could play out whilst he was not there to defend himself. He believed his life would be over if Mary found the letter and took it upon herself to open it. There was nothing else Tom could do, being hundreds of miles away. He decided that the best thing to do was not draw too much attention to the letter.

"You never guess who met me today at the station?

"Go on, who?"

"Do you remember Bob? The detective I worked with and helped train. Well, he lives and works here now. He and his wife have invited me to dinner, which I must admit is a comfort."

"That's lovely to hear, don't go empty-handed you should get some flowers for his wife to say thank you for cooking, especially as it is at the last minute."

Tom agreed it would be a nice gesture. Glancing at his watch, Tom realised he had only a few minutes to get back to the B&B and have a quick wash and brush up.

"Darling, I'm sorry I have to leave you like this; I haven't much time before my driver picks me up to go."

"I understand; you big London detectives lead busy lives." It was nice to hear Mary laugh a little as she said it.

"I love you, darling," she added, hoping that Tom would say the same to her.

"Me too," he replied. Although, he was used to saying how he felt more since he met Mary. It felt awkward to him sometimes. Mary knew this but appreciated the gesture.

Dinner that evening, he was sure, would be interesting for everyone. He had not spoken to Bob in almost ten years at the least. Not since the original case had ended. What were they all going to talk about, definitely not the weather? He knew it would be best not to talk about the case past or present for several reasons, not least of which; he did not want to upset his host's wife. He realised at that moment that he didn't know her name.

Tom thought about the problem until Rabi called to pick him up; when he arrived, Tom greeted him with the statement,

"I bet Bob must be a barrel of laughs still!" Hoping to pry at least a small clue as to how Bob is nowadays at least."

"Would you be if all you did was work on fraud cases all day?"

Rabi hadn't meant to be flippant, he was tired, and it had been a long day for him also, and all he wanted was to drop Tom off at Bob's house and go home.

"Have you met his wife?" Tom asked in another attempt for information. Tom realised at this point tonight was not going to be easy.

"No." Rabi replied, "few people have. We all think she doesn't exist down at the station. You'll be the first to meet her since he got here a few years ago. All we know, he married whilst here on holiday and never went back down south, or so rumour has it.".

They soon arrived at Bob's house; it was ordinary looking, although he did not know what he was expecting. The front garden was concrete with a small, neat flower bed and no gate between the posts that stood as a monument to what had once been there.

Tom stood and gathered his thoughts; before knocking on the front door, he gave a light cough to clear his throat in preparation for the conversation ahead of him. Bob soon great Tom with a welcoming smile. Rabi hung around for a moment, hoping to catch a glimpse of Bob's wife so he could tell everyone back at the station. Tom turned to Rabi, still waiting in the car and waved him off, he knew why Rabi had hung around, but he didn't want to give him the satisfaction.

"Come in; darling Tom's here," Bob said as Tom entered the house "I'll be right there," a voice called out.

Tom smiled as he handed Bob a bottle of wine and said, "Hmm, something smells good! What are we having?" Bob replied with a wry smile and said, "wait and see."

Still clutching the flowers Mary had told him to bring, Tom stood patiently in the living room as Bob disappeared, "back in a moment!" he cried as he left the room. Bob returned to the room moments later. "May I introduce Karen, my wife. Karen, this is Tom. I told you about how we used to work together back in the day.' Karen looked up from her chair directly at Tom and the flowers he was still holding. "Hello Tom, how are you?" Tom found himself just staring. He was not expecting Karen to be in a wheelchair. Tom quickly regained his composure and hoped he had not made it look too obvious; Tom replied.

"It's lovely to meet you. Mary, my wife, suggested I ought to pick these up for you for going to so much trouble and cooking a meal for someone you've never met before." Karen smiled sweetly; her smile reminded him of his wife back home. It was the kind that started from her eyes and finished at her lips.

All Tom's worries and fears soon melted away; she was beguiling and un-hindered at the same time. Karen replied, "Oh, it's no bother. Bob does the cooking; I give him the instructions on what to do, and he does the rest, teamwork."

"Hidden depths a Bob?"

Bob replied quickly, "you haven't tried it yet; it might be awful." Tom smiled again, knowing everything was going to be alright. Well, at least for tonight.

The time passed quickly, and the conversation had been easy without any awkward silence breaks. Karen made her excuses politely to leave "the boys," as she called them, to chat about the good old days. It was clear that this was how the conversation was going, and Karen knew she could not compete, nor would she want to try.

All was going very well until Bob asked, "Do you think our murders here are by the same person from ten years ago?"

Tom was a little taken aback; the direct question was not what he was hoping; still, he replied. "I hope not, but we shall have to see where the evidence leads us." Tom knew he had already said this to Bob today; however, he still believed it to be the best defence.

"What's the evidence saying at the moment?" Bob tried to push just a little more. He was, hoping to get an idea of how Tom was thinking.

"Hmm! It seems almost identical at this stage, but as I say, we'll have to see where the evidence takes us." Tom said, almost perhaps a little too abruptly.

"If you need help, let me know. You know where I am".

"That's kind of you. I appreciate it. We shall see how things go tomorrow; look at the time! I should be getting back; they lock doors if I'm not back by a certain time, where I'm staying."

Tom thanked Bob once again for a lovely evening and asked Bob to pass on his best regards to Karen.

29

Tom was very tired. He knew he would need to settle some things in his mind before sleep, although that is what his body and mind were screaming out to him. Bob offered to call Tom a taxi, but Tom refused and said the fresh air and the walk would help him think clearly.

Standing on the doorstep, Tom thanked Bob once more, and after shaking his hand, he turned to walk away. The air was too cold for Tom as he walked home, well, home of sorts if you call a bedroom in the attic of an old Victorian guest house. *It's better than being in the cellar, who knows what could be stored there! Still, I suppose, it's warm and dry,* he thought.

It was not long before Tom had managed to get himself completely lost and wished he had Rabi driving him back or even the taxi that Bob had offered. It was 11 pm. Tom was growing concerned; the front door of the guest house would be closed in 30 minutes, and he could not be sure which way was home.

In the distance, a little way ahead, he could make out a figure standing in the half-light of the lamp post. As Tom moved closer, he saw a man standing there lighting his cigarette. Tom decided that although this looked very suspicious, he would ask the person for directions hoping for some more northern hospitality. Tom approached with caution, deciding that it would be best not to reveal himself to be a police officer; Tom needed the help and not to try to make an arrest. Instead, he thought it better to inquire under the guess of a lost tourist looking for the guest house on cannery street.

Tom could feel his heart pounding just a little quicker. *Get a grip of yourself, man!* Tom told himself. *You're a police officer, not a boy scout.*

"Evening, Sir," the man standing in the half-light came forward. As Tom got close enough to see, the man swiftly put out the cigarette and moved more into the light. Tom smiled to himself. It was just a bobby on his beat, having a sly smoke to keep warm.

Tom ignored the misdemeanour in favour of some help and assistance to find his way.

The constable realised who Tom was and replied that it was on his rounds, and we were only a ten-minute brisk walk, "I'll walk you there myself." The constable was keen to keep on Tom's right side. Smoking on duty even, in the cold, could mean being written up with a disciplinary added for good measure.

"I saw you with Rabi today. Are you the detective from London who has come to help us with the two murders?"

"Yes, that's me." Tom replied, "some detective getting lost. Still, I suppose you will not be talking about it back at the station when you're next on your break having a well-earned smoke, ah constable?"

"Of course not, sir. I know how to keep a secret and mind my own business." The constable replied. "Well, here we are, sir, safe and sound. Good night, sir. See you around, I'm sure."

"Yes, of course, constable and, thank you. You should, of course, give them up! the cigarettes that is; I'm told, they'll be the death of us all."

"So will this job out in all weathers." The constable replied as he made his farewells and left Tom standing at the door.

As Tom walked into the B&B, he was greeted at the door by Steve, dressed in his pyjamas, slippers, and dressing gown. "Prompt and punctual, that's what I like and would expect from a man of your position and your character," he said as he locked the door.

Tom smiled and agreed by saying, "Prompt and punctual, always on time, always a good motto to live by." Although Tom knew it could have been vastly different.

"Goodnight Tom, see you at breakfast, seven am sharp." And with that, he ascended the stairs to a well-earned sleep.

Chapter Six

Courage, Fortitude, and Tea

Mary could only watch in disbelief as Tom left the house. *What was happening to her family?* Her negative thoughts overwhelmed her mind and heart. *Could Tom solve this mystery. Was he responsible for a tragic miscarriage of justice? Would it ever be possible for her husband to clear his name?* The thought of this weighed heavy on Mary's mind.

Is hanging the right way to discourage and stop people from committing the worst crimes imaginable?

As Mary sank further into her thoughts, her mind began to race with many more questions. *What if, ten years ago, an innocent man was sentenced to death? What would happen to Tom? Could Tom be guilty of murder? Is Barry's conviction entirely down to him? Would Tom go to prison? Worse, could he be hung?*

The questions kept coming one after the other, like the perpetual tide crashing into the shore and rocks slowly eroding away. Eventually, it all became too much for Mary. She pulled out a chair at the kitchen table, where her husband had sat previously and began to cry. Her tears were not just for her but for everyone involved in this whole ghastly mess.

No one could hold her hand, wipe away her tears or make a cup of tea for her as she might have done for others. As she tried to dry her eyes and stop her tears, all she could hear was the sound of the kitchen clock. The ticking marked every second of time, almost taunting her, and made her realise she was all alone until Emily came home from school.

Suddenly out of the corner of her eye, she noticed the small plaque she had once hung in her café. It read *Courage, Fortitude, and Tea.* This sign had always amused her. Mary liked to think that is what helped England win the war and stand against Hitler's bombs during the constant air raids on this green and pleasant land we call home.

Of course, Courage and fortitude were the main qualities needed by everyone during that time. Tea, however, always made everything seem much better; after all, we are British, and that's what we are known for.

Mary picked up the kettle, filled it with plenty of water, and placed it on the stove. She could see the press standing outside, waiting for Tom to come out. Mary knew they would not be going away empty-handed. *I will have to engage them, take the fight to them, and try to control the situation somehow.*

Inspiration seemed to come out of nowhere.

"TEA!" she thought aloud; *that's what I should do! I'll make them tea and give them a nice piece of my homemade cake.* Her thought was interrupted by the whistling sound of the kettle boiling on the stove.

Mary also knew the police, especially the home office, would never comment on any case, past or present. Mary knew this would leave the press to print and say whatever they liked. This would mean they could safely print whatever falsehoods and untruths they wanted, as the police would not prosecute them for fear of revealing the details of specific crimes. If nothing else, it would help them see that her family was strong and not disturbed unduly by what was happening.

Mary went upstairs and fixed her hair and makeup, not that she was accustomed to wearing much. She did not want anybody to see she had been crying and mistake it for self-pity; that would never do. Tom would not want to read that in his morning paper.

Mary returned down the stairs, made several cups of her best tea, and put some pieces of her cake onto a tray. After putting on her best smile, she calmly walked outside to greet the press boys.

"Hello gentlemen, I thought you may require some hot tea and refreshments." Mary was shaking like a leaf inside. She told herself repeatedly, Courage, Fortitude, and tea.

The press boys were silent for a brief while, unsure how to react. They were expecting Tom, someone they knew they could shout questions at in an almost bullish way without fear of reprisal. Instead, this was something different, something they had not expected.

Mary seized her opportunity to remind them that it would be better to speak to Tom.

"I'm very sorry gentlemen, inspector Richards is not here. He will not be back for a few days." Mary said.

"He is working away at the moment on another case." She quickly told herself it was not lying if the two cases were not connected at all.

"Why not enjoy the tea and cake then take a trip to Scotland Yard. I am very sure they can help you better. You know they don't tell us, women, anything. So, you see chaps, I simply cannot help." Mary tried hard to look as innocent as possible and sound like the dutiful housewife, just doing her daily routine.

"Are you Mrs Richards?"

"Yes, Sir, I am."

"Can you tell us anything about your husband's case?"

"We women don't get involved in this sort of thing. It's all far too complicated. I hope you enjoy your tea and cake."

The trick had seemed to be working for the most part. The press finished the tea and cake and drifted away. Mary could not be sure they would go straight to Scotland Yard as requested. She could only hope, but at least they were leaving. Only two of them remained. It was as if they knew she was up to something. They tried to gently probe and asked more general questions. Mostly they asked questions related to how she felt about what was happening but all the time hoping to bring out details of how Tom was thinking and reacting to the murders.

Mary was aware of what they were up to and was far sharper than they had thought.

"As I say, I'm only a housewife, looking after my family and home!"

"I understand, Mrs Richards. Can you tell us what case your husband is working on?"

"Is that not men's work?" she replied to their inquiries.

"I don't even pretend to know what's going on. All I know is that my clever husband is a policeman. He tries his best to keep us all safe and protect us. Of course, You would be much better off talking to him or any of the other nice policemen who work at Scotland yard. I'm sure they know and understand much more than I can about it all."

If the press believed Mary was just the good little housewife, doing the cooking and cleaning. She thought it would be much easier for everyone; this included their daughter Emily. Playing dumb seemed a much safer strategy.

The two gentlemen thanked Mary politely for their refreshments and walked away.

Instinct told them there was a better story to be had. The two remaining reporters knew they would have to be more strategic and plan better. If they wanted to get the story, more work would be involved. After all, they may have lost the battle but not the war!

Chapter Seven

Vultures and manipulators of truth

Tom had often referred to the press as acting like vultures. They wait for the dying moments; they are ready to pick at the juicy flesh to weave it into a story they could sensationalise to increase their circulation.

The truth, he believed it to be, was, when it came to stories like this, don't worry about facts, add in plenty of speculation, and fuel public opinion as much as possible. The public has always had an appetite for true-life murder stories and a good hanging; Tom's story would not be an exception.

Today though, it seems their appetite is becoming less about hanging and more about the rights and wrongs of capital punishment. Could it be that sometimes there are extenuating circumstances?

Bernie, a long-time and well-respected member of the British press, was interested in the real stories. He had never been a fan of capital punishment; he thought it barbaric and a senseless waste of life; this was the story he was after.

He liked to think of himself as the challenger for all who might have met with injustice, those people treated badly and perhaps wrongly convicted and hanged.

Bernie knew that if he were patient, he would get his story, the people's story.

There was a growing dislike for capital punishment as far as he could see. Yes, murder was always going to be wrong; however, even he could see that sometimes circumstances could make a difference.

Bernie knew and understood that some form of punishment was needed, especially for crimes that involve murder. However, he knew even the home office would commute a capital sentence to life in prison when presented with the appropriate background information.

Bernie could see that the home office did not have the will or the stomach to carry out a sentence that could make them look barbaric; we had not long fought and won a war. We were now victors of the down-trodden and heralding in a new era of peace and prosperity.

Bernie needed another gross miscarriage of justice to further his pet cause for justice. Surely this time, he could get his readers and the London Tribune to back a call for a suspension and a full inquiry into the whole idea of capital punishment.

Bernie decided he needed to get Mary onside, get her to let her guard down; that is when the idea hit him, "flowers!" He exclaimed in perhaps what might have seemed too louder voice. Everyone in the office just turned and looked at him.

Everyone called it the office even though it was a little corner booth in the pub just down from Fleet Street. Only Hacks, writers, and their sources would ever frequent there. The air was thick with smoke and testosterone. Internally, the walls were dark brown with green tiles. The ceiling was yellow, possibly from the overbearing smoke and nicotine.

It was easy to tell the serious, committed writers from the hacks; they were the ones who kept themselves apart from everyone else. These writers all had crawled the same streets and news columns to find the best stories to tell. Just like Bernie, it had been their apprenticeship.

Bernie's place, like many others, became his alone, it was his by a right of tenure, and he had earned it through dogged hard work and determination. Many of his colleagues had their places also. The only way it became someone else's would be to leave it in a wooden box, and, even then, it may take some years to get it. Still, until that happened, it was Bernie's, and it was where he sat and thought, he did his best thinking or planning in his office.

Without further hesitation, Bernie gulped down what was left of his beer and headed out the door to the corner. Bernie took a small piece of paper from his pocket and wrote a few simple words. *Thank you for your kind hospitality today; sorry for inconveniencing you. I hope we did not upset you too much. Please accept these flowers as a peace offering. Kindest regards, Bernie; The London Tribune.*

Outside of the pub was a small stall selling flowers. The young woman running it had been there years; it was her mother's before her; this was often the way things went in her line of work.

Bernie picked a conservative bouquet of flowers. Hoping this would be enough to secure an interview at a later stage, he knew and believed in the phrase, *you catch more flies with honey.*

Bernie did not want to give them to Mary in person. He knew if a strange man were to be seen on a married women's doorstep giving her flowers, it would set too many tongues wagging. And damage his chances of getting the story he wanted.

He sent the flowers round to Mary's house using a young lad that was always hanging around looking for odd errands to run for the chance of some small change. Giving him sixpence for his effort and sending him on his way, Bernie reminded him shouting out, "don't forget in-person!" as the young lad took off down the street.

Hopefully, anyone else watching might think it was Bob, who had sent them to his loving wife, waiting patiently at home. Besides, he needed Mary to take the flowers into the house, read his note and accept his apology, and not just throw them straight back at him. Bernie couldn't be sure that this gesture would work; he felt his story was worth the investment in both time and expense. Bernie hoped that if the flowers were successful, she would see him as different to the other reporters and allow him access to the case.

Bernie was sure that he would get the human story if he showed enough patience. The story that can and will affect people's lives, the sort to challenge people's thinking forever and perhaps save lives. Not the headline grabbers that will become tomorrow's fish and chips wrappers.

Chapter Eight

The morning after

Morning came far too quickly for Tom, his alarm waking him at six am. He had not slept well that night, despite being exhausted from the day before. There was far too much to think about, case notes firmly fixed in his mind, along with the pictures he had seen, and the case notes he had read yesterday.

Moreover, spending time away from Mary and his daughter Emily made him feel too uneasy. The strange surroundings, including his bed and not knowing what might happen, made him feel uncomfortable.

By 7 am Tom, was dressed and downstairs ready; he told himself *at least breakfast would be something nice to look forward to and enjoy.* Tom sat at a table near the window; he picked up a complimentary copy of the Daily Mirror. It was not his usual paper, but it did make him feel quite at home. The headline read, "The Russians plan to get there first." Tom found the article quite absorbing and had not realised his breakfast was ready and in front of him.

Fumbling from his paper to his tea and back again. Tom ignored the food until the landlord pointed it out. "Do you not like porridge, Mr Richards?" Tom looked up from his paper, smiled and replied, "I'm sorry I haven't tried it. I was quite engrossed in this story about going to space."

"Do you think it's possible?" the landlord replied.

"I'm sure the British, Americans or maybe the Russians will, although I don't know why!" Tom looked down at his porridge, took a spoon and put a small amount into his mouth. Tom coughed and screwed his face up, forgetting where he was for a moment, blurted, "urgh! It's salty."

"Yes, Mr Richards, that's how we Scott's eat our porridge, just as the good Lord intended."

"I'm Sorry, down south, we use sugar or honey if we can get it. Is it possible to get some toast with marmalade?" Tom asked.

"No!" the landlord said quite firmly "it's almost 8 am, and the kitchen will be closed,"

Tom could only look on in silence and disbelief at the attitude and inflexibility of his host. He restrained himself with a smile and replied. "No problem." He saw Rabi arriving to take him back to the station and saw it as an opportunity to make a quick exit without causing a further disturbance.

Rabi was looking quite pensive; he was not sure what the day would bring; he could tell that it may well be interesting by the look on Tom's face as he approached the car.

"Morning, Sir," Rabi said, "good night last night, was it?" hoping not just to make polite conversation but to also pry any gossip out.

"Morning Rabi does the station serve toast with marmalade?" Tom asked rather abruptly.

"Yes, sir, well, at least I think so," replied Rabi in a confused voice.

"Then that's our first port of call."

Tom and Rabi soon arrived at the station without any further conversation on the way.

"Tea and marmalade toast, that's the way to get the morning started!" Tom revealed a small insight into his routine and perhaps a little about himself with his statement. Tom asked the lady at the counter for two pots of tea and two lots of toast with marmalade, collecting and paying for his breakfast, and he left the canteen for his office.

Rabi was left asking himself what he should do, should he follow Tom or report back to his chief; *if I were to do the latter, what would I say? He asked himself.* The decision was soon not his any longer. Another constable soon arrived to summon both he and Tom to the chief's office. He wanted an update and an initial plan of action, including Tom's thoughts on what he had already learned about the case.

"Can you please tell the chief we will both be there presently? Tom has something he has to do first!"

Rabi did not want to explain that Tom had taken his breakfast to his office. Tom had not said much regarding the case nor presented his plan of action to Rabi.

Rabi headed to Tom's office to let him know the chief wanted an update. "Glad you're here, Rabi, you should have some toast and tea whilst it's still hot."

"Sir, should we not be going to see the chief?"

"No! Rabi, he can wait till I have had my breakfast. Come on and help yourself."

Rabi was not sure how to react. Or what to make of Tom's attitude. He had never witnessed anyone ignore the chief before. It wasn't long before they finished eating. "You see, Rabi, breakfast is important in our job. Now let's go and see what the chief has to say."

Rabi smiled and brushed the crumbs from his jacket before they left to see the chief.

"Right, Tom, what's your verdict so far?" the chief asked in his usual brashness. Tom thought for a few moments before answering.

"At this stage of my inquiry, it would be very wrong to assume the murderer is the same person or persons. I have only seen several photographs of the two girls and read a few reports and statements. I would need to have my original notes back. I need to compare them with each other. Furthermore, I will need to interview anyone related to this case, including anyone that may have encountered the two women in the hours before their death. All of this will help me build a picture of their lives, including lifestyle, habits, friends, did they work, and if so, where? And when and for how long? Were they married, single or engaged? What possible motives could anyone have for killing them? Were they involved with criminal activity?"

Tom stopped, took a breath for a moment, and said, "of course, the girl's deaths here do have a link with those from the past!"

The chief interrupted Tom, "so they are by the same person?"

Tom looked at him. "I said they are linked, sir, although, at this stage, it is too early to say with conviction and certainty how. I will need to investigate further, and that, I'm sorry to say, will take time. For now, I would appreciate my notes back, and if possible, I would like Rabi to take me to the site where the girls were found."

"You don't want much, do you?"

"I need to make sure, Sir, that I do my job to the best of my abilities and get them justice; these two girls deserve that at least."

"That's very true, Tom. Make sure you do!"

"I am quite sure of one thing, sir; I will be out most of today. I can give you a better update in the morning if that helps?" Tom was determined not to be bullied this morning and took a more decisive stand.

Rabi just kept silent; he had never seen anyone stand up to the chief in this way before.

The chief looked a little shocked at Tom's direct approach; he had not had anyone speak to him like this before; in his mind, he admired Tom for this but would not say.

The chief allowed a few moments of silence before handing the case notes back to him. He was still in charge and wanted to reinforce that with Tom. Tom's face was expressionless; it was impossible to say what he was thinking. Tom took his files from the chief, said thank you and left the room.

"Come on, time to go. I want to see the dumpsites, Rabi." Tom said as he walked down the corridor. Rabi followed in hot pursuit. He thought *this might get exciting; at the very least, I may not get another opportunity like this again.*

It was not long before they arrived at the first of the *dumpsites.* Tom had eloquently phrased it earlier.

The girl's bodies had already been removed and taken to the morgue. Rabi was confused by this. What could Tom gain from visiting himself after the fact? He kept his thoughts to himself and paid close attention. This was his opportunity to learn from a famous London detective, who knows maybe even his picture in the newspaper or perhaps a promotion, and one day become a detective himself. His thoughts and imagination began to run away with him.

Tom never said a word at first. He just kept staring at the ground, then at the first picture of the body, and then back to his original case pictures.

Although Tom had been confident back at the station with the chief, he certainly was not here. Always the question, what if he got it wrong?

Rabi was not sure how to help Tom. He kept quiet and watched until all that was happening was Tom standing, staring at the pictures of the two victims. One photo in each hand, two different victims year's apart.

"What do you notice about these two pictures Rabi? Take a close look and say aloud what you see, don't miss a single detail." Tom wanted Rabi involved as much as possible, initially as a second pair of eyes but also as a sounding board for ideas.

Rabi, somewhat nervous, looked down at the two pictures; neither looked pleasant to him, but this was now his job.

Hesitating, Rabi began at first to speak softly and said, "I see...I see a picture of a woman lying on her back. Her face is covered, covered with a white handkerchief,"

"Yes! Go on, what else do you see?" Tom asked.

"The picture looks the same as the second, except it's different. In the first photo, the girl's arms a crossed against her chest, but it's not the same in the second photo," Rabi replied. He had gained some confidence and continued.

"Also, in the first photo, the handkerchief is set differently. The handkerchief is not square on the girls' face; it's angled more like a diamond."

"Exactly, well done. In the original case, the handkerchiefs on the girl's, were set as diamonds, and both victims' arms crossed over their chests as if they were ready for burial. At the time of the first two murders, we thought the handkerchiefs were symbolic. We knew it was important to the killer,"

Tom was now quite excited; he knew the case was different; all he now needed to do, was follow the clues. Tom began to make notes, his mind racing with so many questions, still so much to do. One thing was now very sure to Tom; he had not been wrong, and this was a new case, with many similarities granted, but a new and different case, nonetheless.

Tom looked up at Rabi, smiled, and said. "I believe we have our first breakthrough. Don't talk to anyone until we can be sure, not to friends, family and especially colleagues. We don't know who is involved or connected; this must stay with us, are you clear?" Rabi just nodded his head. "Don't just nod your head; swear to me now!"

Rabi stared straight at Tom and replied, "Yes, of course I won't say a word to anyone."

"What do we need to do now, sir?"

"We need to build up a picture of the girls' lives, check if they were connected, do they have friends in common, do they work, and if so, where? Do they have hobbies, are they sociable, where do the girls both go? and who do they see? Are they honest or dishonest? Do they live alone, at home, with friends? How much money do they have, or do they owe money? If that is the case, how much and to whom? No stone unturned and no questions left unanswered."

Tom knew he had to talk to the chief about all of this. After all, since he knew this was not the same murderer any longer and an entirely different case, albeit with some similar circumstances. Tom knew he might not be allowed to continue with the investigation and take the lead. His thoughts quickly turned to his wife and daughter back home. *Could this mean I will be going home as early as tonight?* He thought.

Somehow though, Tom knew he could not be lucky enough to catch two breaks in one day. Once more, his mood began to drop at the prospect of having to stay and finish the investigation.

The investigation was not his, but he knew it does not always work like that; his breakthrough was still conjecture and theory he had yet to convince his boss back home and the chief here. It was at that point it hit him.

If the two murders are not connected, why go to all the trouble of making it look like they were? And why copy his case? Come to think of it, how did they know enough to make it look like they were?

As Tom began to worry, more questions came to mind. First, *who knows that much detail? Not the public. Second, was it personal; was someone trying to make him look bad or just trying to mislead this investigation?*

Chapter Nine

The update

Tom could not think of any reason someone would want to ruin his reputation. Why go to such great lengths and commit murder? Twice?

Tom mussed with his thoughts; it is not paranoia if it is true. If it were, he would still have to prove it and show motive for anyone to take notice of him.

Tom had never thought of himself as paranoid before, cautious perhaps but never paranoid. Now it might seem that he would have to be quite guarded in his speech and actions. He knew if treachery were to blame, it would have to be someone connected to him.

The chief had been out all afternoon at an important event; this meant he could not be disturbed, even by Tom, wanting to give him an update.

That night Tom could hardly sleep, his thoughts echoing loud in his mind, constant in their message. He had upset someone to make them discredit him in such a way.

Sleep rarely came easy to Tom when he was on an investigation, but now it had seemed an impossibility. His body cried out, desperate for some respite.

This case was already taking a toll on him physically and mentally; without anyone to talk to, Tom was all alone. Tom began to make plans for the morning, plans on whom he was going to tell and what details to tell, it was not going to be easy, but for now, he thought the least said the better.

Deciding that to work the case properly, he would tell the chief he would have to run two investigations parallel to each other headed by one person. Tom!

At that very moment, Tom had decided he would need to see this through; this was his investigation and no one else's; someone had involved him from the start. Tom may not know who or why, but one thing was sure; he would find out.

The morning came quick enough, he knew he had some sleep but not so much that would make a difference, he was on a mission.

Tom showered, changed, and left before his alarm had gone off; he was not waiting for that gruesome salty porridge or his usual cup of tea.

Tom burst into the chief's office with a renewed confidence to update him with his version of events; "sir" he said, "this is what I have for you right now." He went on to explain that although he was convinced the Scottish murders were separate from the London murders, he could not in all honesty say why at this stage and believes he should stay here to investigate further.

The chief asked why he should allow this and what convinced him to follow this theory.

Tom declined politely but firmly saying "it would be better to keep this information to myself just a little while longer; twenty-four hours at the very least."

The chief reluctantly agreed to his demands adding, "twenty-four hours it is, then I want all your findings."

Tom was happy at this although a little worried he had not meant to give himself such a short time like that, the deal had been struck there was no going back.

By the time he got to the briefing room, it was full of uniforms waiting to find out their jobs for their shift.

Rabi had done a great job collecting people to help them; some would go door to door, others talking to the public to see who knew the girls. Tom and Rabbi were to interview the girl's families; this needed a sensitive touch, not Bobbies from their beat.

It was not long before information began to pour in; a picture was now forming about the two female victims:

The victims were not related to each other; the only way they were connected was that they both had worked as waitresses at a private gentleman's club. The club had been a well-established society with a long-standing reputation as a place where real business took place over scotch and cigars.

The only way to gain entrance was an invitation; you only received an invitation if you're a somebody.

Tom understood about such clubs as London had many similar places; not that he nor anyone he knew could ever have a cause or reason to visit, let alone be invited.

This news began to worry Tom; the only person he knew that could belong to such an organisation was the chief and perhaps other high-ranking officers.

He knew he was going to have to tread very carefully. The last thing he needed right now was to have them against him. It was all too clear. Tom would need a way to reassure the chief, he was going to be careful and not make wild accusations at any members. He also knew that to do his job properly, he would have to follow wherever the clues lead him even if that meant going into the lion's pit.

Tom began to formulate a plan; he would leave out the information about the club for the time being and concentrate on how and where the girls had died.

Chapter Ten

The investigation

Back at their office, Tom and Rabi began to comb through the reports on the girls.

"It's important, Rabi, take care and look at every detail carefully."

"O.k. Sir, I will."

"Every detail will tell us a part of the girl's story."

"Sir, I notice that our two girls have a lot of bruising with large bruises on their necks. What do you think? And this report says there were signs of sexual assault."

"Let me see, Rabi; this is significant to the case and very different from my original murder case; there were no signs of bruising, even though they had been sexually assaulted, however, their eyes had been removed."

"Why were their eyes missing, sir?"

"That's a good question, Rabi. We believe this was for more psychotic reasons and not because of power or violence. The victims were well cared for, and as I said earlier, no bruising or signs of struggle."

As Tom looked more intently at the pictures of the girls, he asked Rabi, "What do you make of the bruising around the girl's necks?"

"I'm not sure, sir, but it does look like a handprint, I suppose."

"That's what I was thinking; I'd say a large hand, wouldn't you?"

"Yep, I think your right."

It was generally known and accepted by the experts that only men assault girls in this way, thus confirming suspicions that it was a man who had killed them.

"I think this could be a large thumbprint bruise! Rabi, I now believe that we are looking for one male person; with large, strong, build and large hands, and since both girls have a connection to the club, we should concentrate our efforts and resources on investigating all members, including the staff."

Rabi was surprised at how quickly things could change in this investigation, but he was determined to keep up and continue to assist in any way he could.

Tom and Rabi would need more information as that description could fit too many people, including the chief.

They now decided to look more closely at the reports and information from the public; maybe someone had been interviewed that matched this description. In any case, it would help to build a picture of their lives.

Questions still needed to be answered, what were the girls like as people? Both girls were only seventeen and still living at home. Neither of them had any real steady work until the gentleman's club allowed them to be employed, on a part-time basis, evenings only.

Other similarities had begun to emerge from the door-to-door investigation; both were not always the most stable people in terms of reliability and common sense. Their school reports often spoke of the pair of them both being a little naïve and perhaps easily led by others into situations they would not necessarily choose for themselves.

Neither of the girls had many real friends, often choosing their own company away from their families. Although neither of them had any money problems, they had never really seemed to have enough for the week. All this changed about two weeks before their death when both had begun buying clothes and makeup. Often, being seen around the city more, in and out of restaurants.

It had become noticeably clear the girls had found themselves in a situation they had not been looking for, or perhaps they had been flattered by the extra income and attention. Maybe they had attracted the attention of someone with evil intentions, a predator who recognised their vulnerabilities and prayed on this with flattery and the promise of more exciting times ahead.

Maybe it was a simple explanation. Perhaps the girls were just in the wrong place at the wrong time.

In either case, neither deserved their outcomes; to be murdered and tossed aside like rubbish as if no one cared for them. The truth is there are always people who care enough. If not relatives or friends, he would care enough to find justice and try and make a difference in the lives of people who seemed to have none.

This case was no longer about himself or his reputation. It was about all victims of crime and the reasons he joined the force in the first place, for it was not just to serve and protect but to investigate and find answers for those left behind, to ensure those who were guilty were caught and punished and most importantly it was about the victims themselves having a voice. A voice long after they were gone.

To this end, Tom dug deep into his experience and mental strength. He wanted to catch this menace to society and women in particular. This thought spurred him to work harder and use every resource available, including Rabi, a constable who seemed keen to learn and assist him on every step. At this moment, he remembered Jane; she would have the connections he might need, especially at the club where her help could prove invaluable. Tom knew he needed to follow with an air of caution in more ways than one; after all, Jane, he was sure, probably now thought that he had ignored her letter and also her.

How would he approach Jane after all this time or ask for her help? Would she receive him courteously or push him away for not replying to her? He thought to himself.

"Keep mum!" Tom said out loud. This slogan from the war hit home hard with him. He knew that the information he and Rabi now had needed to be kept to them only.

"Remember, Rabi! This information doesn't leave this room; it stays only with us."

"Yes, I remember, sir. I won't say anything to anyone."

To Tom, mum meant something extra; the American spelling of mum is, mom; for him, these were the initials for Motive, Opportunity and Means. He needed to establish all three to get a successful conviction once he caught the killer.

Right now, though, he needed to focus on establishing his prime suspects, and at this moment in time, he had none, even though he thought the answer lay inside the club.

"Rabi!" Tom called, "we need to go to the club and speak with the manager to build more of a picture of the two girls. Will you please drive me?"

"Yes, of course. I'll bring the car around now."

Tom waited by the front entrance hoping to meet the PC from the previous night, which more by luck than judgement happened.

"Hello, Sir. How are you today?"

"I'm very well constable. How do you feel about using that discretion you told me about last night and helping me?"

"What do you have in mind, sir?"

Speaking quietly to him, Tom asked, "I would like you to make inquiries at the back of a particular gentleman's club on your beat. It needs complete discretion. I would like you to speak with all the staff, as many as you can and find out if anything unusual has been happening lately, big, or small, take careful note of everything."

"Yes, sir, I know the club."

"See if anyone knew the girls and their reputation. The girls must have spoken with others there, even if all they did was gossip."

"What about my usual duties, sir?"

"I will square it with the chief, don't worry."

Tom knew that back-door gossip was rife in any large establishment; he also knew that if the staff were to be officially interviewed by his team, then silence would ensue as there could be dangerous repercussions for everyone.

"You know your beat well, but if I can make a suggestion, try to go softly, perhaps see if there's a cup of tea going first for a poor bobby on the beat."

The P.C agreed to Tom's request and immediately set off for the club. Tom never mentioned this to Rabi, preferring to keep this to himself for the time being.

Tom's latest recruit had seemed keen to help and didn't waste time getting to the club. The young P.C introduced himself, "Hi, my name is George. I'm your new neighbourhood copper." He said with a friendly smile to the woman sitting on a crate having a smoke.

"Mind if I join you?" he asked, convincing himself it would be O.K. as it was in the line of duty.

"Help yourself!" she replied, "it's a free country."

"To tell you the truth. I was hoping to get a quick cuppa and thought you might oblige me."

"Well, you're not slow at coming forward, are you, George? I'll take you through to the kitchen."

The kitchen was very busy with people everywhere; pots and pans clattering; it was a little overwhelming.

George was grateful for the tea, "shall we step back outside and leave them to it?" he suggested.

Once outside, he gently probed the woman about the two girls, asking if she knew them.

The woman was reluctant to talk; she would only say that both girls were young, easily led and liked a party.

"Did they go to many parties?" George enquired further.

The woman nodded and turned away; she no longer wanted to discuss this further. A work college called her asking when her break was over. She turned to George and said, "I've got to go now. You need to talk to James, but I never said!"

George decided that he didn't want to look too suspicious or overstay his welcome and chose to return to the station to report his findings.

Chapter Eleven

Jane, 1944

Jane is a real lady of title, her father an English Lord (although referred to as Laird) with land in Scotland and a family tree tracing their routes back through many centuries. The connections he could boast in business and socially would mean she would be heir to a fortune and have a marriage alliance worthy of royalty; a tall, elegant lady with impeccable manners and graciousness; a lady who could astound you with her down-to-earth, caring attitude and beauty.

It was 1944 when Jane met Tom; he was visiting a local hospital where she had been working. Tom was there making inquiries regarding a murder case of particular gruesomeness. Jane was not the person he was there to meet; however, he could not help but notice her beauty and gracious manner with the patients and their relatives.

"Hello, my name is Inspector Richards of Scotland yard. Could you please remind me of the name of the doctor I was talking to?" He asked with a warm smile.

Jane smiled in return and replied, "DR Harris, is there anything else I could do for you?"

"Yes, I require more information, and Doctor Harris seemed reluctant to talk perhaps because he is busy, I would presume."

Jane looked up at him; all she could see were his big brown eyes and a lovely smile. "I am rather busy myself. However, I am due for a break soon and would be happy to help you over a cup of tea." Jane replied, hoping not to seem too eagerly interested in him.

Tom instinctively knew something had just happened; he was not too familiar with that feeling but knew all the same that something exciting was about to begin.

Tom took the opportunity to meet with her and replied with the same eagerness she had shown him, "yes, that would be great. Should I meet you here?" Tom asked.

"No, there's a small café near the entrance to the hospital, you can't miss it. I'll meet you there in twenty minutes." Then before anyone could change their minds or an awkward silence fell upon them both, Jane was called away to help with a patient brought directly in from the battle of Arnhem.

"Nurse, can you please remove the bandages so that I might make a better examination of him?" the doctor asked.

Jane apprehensively moved closer; the man had been badly burned the bandages applied earlier were now sticking to the wounds. Jane knew this would be excruciating pain for him and perhaps a little traumatic for her at best. Jane moved closer to him, his eyes staring straight at hers as if he already knew how agonising this would be.

"On second thoughts. I believe a more specialised burns hospital would be best for this patient."

Jane wasn't sure who was more relieved; she knew it meant only temporary relief for him. For now, though, the look on both Jane's and the soldier's eyes told the true story, relief. Jane thanked the soldier for his sacrifice and service and hurried out of the room before anyone noticed how relieved she was.

Jane's attention had moved from meeting Tom to rushing to the nurse's room before anyone saw her crying for what she had just seen and the sacrifice that so many men had made for liberty and freedom. Jane had worked here for some time, and although she had witnessed many atrocities, the man's eyes speaking out in terror and pain touched her heart. Jane remembered the brown eyes of inspector Richards, his smile and the promise to meet him at the café. Jane rushed outside in a panic; she hated the thought of letting someone down.

"I'm so sorry it's not been a great morning. Thank you for waiting."

"That's ok. I'm sorry, I didn't catch your name?"

"Jane." She said, trying hard to catch her breath,

"Thank you, Jane, for meeting me. Are you ok? your eyes look a little red."

"Yes, as I said earlier, it's been a difficult morning, and my last patient; his situation got the better of me."

Jane did not want to go into too much detail and preferred to keep things lighter.

Tom smiled again at her trying to put her at ease.

"Don't worry too much, Jane. I'm sure the war cannot go on much longer."

"I do hope not, inspector."

"Call me Tom; Inspector sounds far too formal."

Although Tom had every good intention of keeping it professional to continue with his investigation, he soon found that the conversation had diverted and was now more about every subject they could think of, including that they both lived alone and were not in a relationship with anyone else.

Tom and Jane felt taken by surprise neither had the intention or thoughts of meeting someone with qualities they could both admire that morning.

Time soon passed, Jane was needed back at work, and Tom was in the middle of a murder investigation; Neither had the time to idle gossip, especially Tom. His case was hitting the headlines almost daily and often front page. He had to catch his man soon; the pressure was mounting.

They both, politely, made their farewells and went their separate ways, neither making any arrangement to meet up again and certainly, not swapping personal details for any future liaison.

It would be three weeks after this meeting before they met again, purely by chance. Almost instinctively, Tom knew he would see her again. For now, though, they both knew they had jobs to do; that was more important at the time.

After meeting for the second time, Tom and Jane knew they were kindred spirits. They made arrangements to meet regularly, when possible, for afternoon tea and some occasions, dinner in the evening.

This arrangement was not a romance of passion, as was now becoming more popular due to the war, but a meeting of minds and hearts, each respecting the other in thought and deed but all the time never really admitting to each other how they felt.

Jane knew that her background would not let her be so forward and tell Tom exactly how she felt; her every thought was for Tom, if only he would declare to her how he felt, she would give up her title, position, and money; for her, these things didn't matter. To Tom, this seemed to weigh heavily on his mind and would prevent him from saying a word. He didn't want to be the one who took her away from her life. *What could he offer Jane?* He thought. A policeman's wage was not much by her standards; as a London detective, he worked long hours and often at inconvenient times.

To Jane, this didn't matter; she was in love with a man she respected and admired. He was not like the men of her station in life, fortune, and position. These were not his goals; helping other people to find justice. His beautiful eyes, smile and personality, were all she wanted; the rest they could figure out later. It seemed that this was not going to be each never really saying how they felt, neither of them showing the bravery they admired in other people.

Time passed by so quickly. Days turned into weeks which, in turn, became months, despite the many horrors and terrible things they had both witnessed, each consoling the other and helping them through. There were sad times and happy times for them both, spending every moment possible in each other's company and always hoping this would never end.

Eventually, the war ended, and Jane was to return to Edinburgh; the last few months for them both had been a journey of discovery; neither had wanted this to end.

Tom drove Jane to the station, the silence from them both saying everything but not saying what they should.

It was night, the clouds heavy with the promise of rain.

Tom and Jane stood on the platform edge holding each other's hand; she was the greatest love of his life. If only he could somehow find a way to tell Jane how much he feels about her, then perhaps she might decide to stay. Time was running out for them both; she would leave for Scotland and almost certainly be out of his life forever. He needed to say something; if he did not say something, then soon it would be too late.

Chapter Twelve

Rabi and the chief

The chief was on the prowl and wanted to know what was happening and had decided Rabi would be his target. Rabi was unaware that the chief was looking for him until he turned a corner and almost bumped into him.

"Oops! Sorry sir, I didn't see you there."

The chief wasn't amused or in the mood for messing around, come to think of it, he never liked any messing around. He was always a straight-talking, get-to-the-point person.

"Rabi," he said in a commanding voice, "I need to see you in my office, now!"

Rabi was a little unnerved by this. However, he thought nothing would spoil his day; he had a secret mission from Tom and was determined to see it through.

Once inside the chief's office, the atmosphere changed, "Close the door, Rabi and take a seat." The chief was trying hard to show a softer, more friendly side which took Rabi by surprise.

"What can I do for you, sir?"

"that's a good question, do you like working with Richards?" he asked, seeming to ignore Rabi's question.

"Yes, sir, very much" at that moment, he paused; what's the chief up to, he thought to himself? Should he tell the boss that inspector Richards is a great guy and knew his stuff, or stay silent and see how this conversation plays out?

"That's good to hear, would you like to continue working with him?"

"Yes, I would like to see how the investigation goes, maybe learn a thing or two from him." Rabi was keen to stay on track; he didn't want to be pulled off the case.

"Perhaps then, you might be able to help me and the station out. We want you to stay helping him, but we need your help."

This conversation intrigued Rabi while making him a little nervous about what he was asking him to do?

"So, it's agreed then Rabi, you'll report back to me every day with all progress and any information no matter how small a detail?"

Rabi hesitated to reply for a moment, which gave the chief time to push harder, "unless of course you like being in uniform and don't have any desire to climb the ranks."

This was a veiled threat and wasn't well-received; he knew he had to reply positively, but he was stuck.

Saying no to the chief could cost him any dreams of becoming a detective but spying on the case didn't seem right.

His mind racing, Rabi agreed and told the chief about his career hopes and aspirations.

"Then, this will be a good place to start; consider it to be you're training." The chief shook Rabi by the hand, which he had never seen before, telling him to "keep this between ourselves."

"Whilst I think about it, do you have anything to tell me now?" Rabi's heart sank; he wasn't sure what to do; he liked Tom, he had been fair to him, and now this felt like a betrayal.

There was an awkward silence that fell upon the room; neither spoke. The chief was good at this game and could wait all day if he had to. What's more, he could use his natural presence and foreboding body language to apply pressure, which is just what he did.

Rabi cracked a little and began to tell his boss some of what he knew. He had heard that there was a woman at the club. Who, through a Bobby on the beat, told Tom that the girls had a particular reputation. They liked going to parties. Rabi believed this information would get him off the hook as he didn't know who said what, although he had a fair idea.

The chief seemed satisfied by his reply but still wasn't saying much. Rabi knew one thing; he wasn't going to tell of his secret mission from Tom. He still had some integrity and believed in loyalty.

"Is there anything else you'd like to share?" He replied, trying to coax information. *Did the chief know more and was looking for confirmation?* He could not be sure, so he wanted to play him at his own game, "sorry sir, perhaps you could be more specific."

"you'll have to be better at your daily briefing Rabi if you want promotion in the future. Are you trying to hide anything from me, something important I should know?"

Rabi was more worried than ever now, trying to think on his feet quickly. He wasn't prepared for such a grilling; Rabi knew he was losing a battle fast but wasn't entirely sure what this battle was or even how to win if he ever could.

After all, he decided that the chief was his boss, and when all was said and done, Tom would eventually go back home to London, his job, wife, and family. On the other hand, he would stay here picking up any pieces of his career if at all there was one.

Slowly, Rabi began to tell him all he knew about the case, including gossip from the canteen. The rumour was that the woman from earlier had mentioned a name, someone to talk to, although he did not include that information. He also related how he had seen George coming out of Tom's office.

As Rabi began to give a full report on what he knew, he found himself letting on about his secret mission. He had made a start; however, it wasn't easy as he had been warned not to go anywhere near the club.

The chief was particularly interested in this significant news flash. Rabi couldn't believe he had just told his boss all about this; more importantly, it was easy to say once he started.

The chief then looked him straight in the eyes and asked, "do you think he is keeping you out of the loop?" Rabi was shocked; this thought made sense to him. Tom was also playing a game here, with secret assignments using other people on the investigation, not letting others see the whole picture.

Rabi now felt a mixture of feelings and emotions. There was a sick feeling in the pit of his stomach. This feeling turned to anger, and on top of it all, he now felt incensed at Tom for treating him this way.

He didn't feel so bad now telling his boss the whole story as he knew it; after all, the chief had helped him realise that Tom wasn't such a nice guy.

Rabi was now more determined than ever to be loyal to the chief and spy on Tom as much as possible, feeding back all progress as soon as possible. Rabi left that room feeling used by Tom, his head spinning, trying to work out what to do, searching for the right way to move forward.

Tom spotted Rabi down the corridor, "Rabi, is there any chance we can have a word?" Rabi's heart began to pound. Had Tom spotted him coming out of the chief's office? Had someone told him that he was even in there

Rabi tried not to look concerned as Tom caught up with him.

"Is everything all right?" he asked, "how are you getting on with the list?"

Tom knew he had not had much time since he had asked Rabi to do this; he conversed politely before asking Rabi the real question.

"Was he in a good mood?" he asked.

"Who sir?"

"The chief, I saw you coming out of his room, I hope he's not taking you away from me, your integral to the case now Rabi."

Rabi looked at him and said, "no, he was just checking that I'm still happy driving you around and running errands for you, that sort of thing."

Rabi couldn't believe he was now lying to a senior officer to protect his skin and hide the real reason why he had been in there.

"Oh, what did you say? Did you tell him that you're my right-hand man and my driver? You do still want to work on this case with me, don't you?"

"Well sir, I told him you were a hard taskmaster, and not only did I want to not work with you anymore, but I also told him I want a transfer to a different station."

Rabi couldn't believe the person he had become in such a short time. Now he was using over-familiar speech, including jokes, to hide what was happening; he almost didn't recognise himself.

Tom smiled and said, "excellent, glad to hear you're happy."

Tom wasn't fooled. He'd seen this behaviour before; something was up; he knew Rabi was overcompensating, trying to hide what was happening.

As they both walked back to Tom's office, they could hear the phone ringing; Rabi rushed forward to answer it, again trying to be extra helpful. "It's for you, sir."

"Thank you, Rabi. Hello, inspector Richards speaking!"

Rabi tried hard to listen to the conversation, but he couldn't understand what was being said. The voice was too faint for him to hear.

Tom turned to Rabi, "that'll be all for now," he said, trying to dismiss him firmly but politely.

Chapter Thirteen

Bob's story

"Sir, is there anything else you need?"

"Thanks, Bob. I do have a couple leads I will need you to check for me."

"No problems, fire away."

Although a recent recruit to the police force, Bob was keen to impress Tom, his new boss. Bob had been a soldier but was discharged due to an injury sustained during the war.

"How's your leg holding up, Bob?"

"Not bad, Sir, it still gives me gip from time to time, but I'll live, I'm sure."

"That's the spirit, although you should say if it gets too much, we can't have our heroes being overloaded."

"Thanks, sir, but I'll be fine."

Bob had taken a bullet in his thigh; at twenty-two, he felt he had so much more to give and at times felt disappointed not to be in the thick of it all fighting for his country. He joined the force after his discharge to help make a difference at home, although he had never expected to be trained as a detective. It had been decided that due to his injury and heroic efforts, he should be fast tract into this position by the higher powers.

Tom could see Bob was keen to get on and learn all he could from him; although Tom never enjoyed the attention Bob gave him, he did, however, respect him and all he had done. Tom would often give Bob extra errands and leads to follow up on, which on some occasions made things a little worse for Bob as some in the team began to tease Bob about it, all in the name of banter.

The war ended, and life returned to a new routine; everyone knew life would never be the same again. However, life did go on, and that was more important. The case Tom had been working on whilst guiding Bob had come to fruition. The murderer had been tried and sentenced when Bob decided it was time to take a well-earned break; *a holiday in Scotland*, he thought to himself, *that's just what I need.*

After arriving in Edinburgh, Bob found himself the perfect Bed and Breakfast to stay in.

"Hello, my name is Karen; how can I help you today?"

Bob was utterly enchanted by her soft Scottish accent and beautiful smile, almost forgetting to speak.

"I'm sorry, Karen, my name is Bob. I would like a room for a few days, please."

"You're in luck, Bob. We have a room available for you; how many nights do you require?"

Karen tried hard to be professional; she was intrigued by Bob's accent.

"I think four nights, please."

"Are you from London, Bob?"

"Yes, that's right, you have a good ear for accents."

Bob was hoping to keep her talking more.

"Thank you, have you been to Edinburgh before?"

"No, I have never even been to Scotland before; I saw a postcard of Edinburgh during the war when I was stationed in France and knew I had to visit."

"Have you recently been demobbed?"

"No, I was injured and discharged; I now work for the London Police force."

"Wow! A hero and a policeman keeping us all safe."

"Well, I'm a detective, so I do my best."

Bob tried hard to impress Karen but didn't want to look like he was boasting. On the other hand, Karen was aware of this and played into his hands just enough to keep him interested in her.

"Is this your house, Karen?"

"No, it's my parents, they are out now, shopping, I think! Here are the keys to your room at the top of the stairs in front of you. To the left of your room is the bathroom. I should not keep you any longer; you're probably tired from your long journey."

"Thank you, Karen, your very kind." Bob smiled as he left, hoping to speak with her again.

Bob took every opportunity to talk with her over the next few days; Karen enjoyed the attention but would not let on too much.

"Karen, I was thinking about going for a picnic today. Would you like to accompany me?"

"I'm not sure that's entirely appropriate, Bob; what would people say?"

"Let them talk; my experience is, if they talk about me, they are leaving someone else alone."

"That's a nice thought, Bob, but!"

"No but's, Karen, it's a lovely day. At least come for a walk with me for an hour or two?"

"Just a walk then, nothing else; I have a reputation to keep up."

"Fair enough, I understand. Can you be ready in an hour?"

"Yes, no problems; I've a few jobs to sort first."

"Excellent." Bob's persistence had finally paid off.

The Walk went well; Karen and Bob enjoyed laughing and talking; it was as if they had long been friends.

"Bob, can I ask you a question?"

"Yes, you can ask me anything, within reason!"

"Are you looking for a holiday romance?"

Bob was surprised at Karen's forwardness; he had not expected that question.

"Why do you ask that?"

"Confusion!"

"What confusion?"

"I'm not sure, but why do you keep answering my question with another?"

"Sorry, professional habit I suppose."

"The answer is no! I'm not looking for a holiday girlfriend, the truth is, I wasn't looking for any romance until I met you."

Karen wasn't sure how to reply; she liked Bob a lot and didn't want to scare him off or be taken for a fool.

"Maybe we should see how it goes." she said politely, hoping it would be enough.

"That's a good plan, if you want, as long as I can come back again to see you."

Karen smiled; that's exactly what she wanted to hear.

Bob visited a few times over the next few months, and they fell in love a little more every time he did.

Eventually, Bob proposed to Karen and made plans to transfer to Edinburgh police before they were married.

Bob knew the wedding plans only concerned him when there was a job to do, everything else Karen and her mum organised. Except that is the honeymoon. Bob saved a little harder to afford a few days away in a small cottage in the picturesque village of Culross. About an hour from the city where the cobbled streets lead you past many 17ths and 18th-century red-tile-roofed buildings. The town boasted a palace and period gardens, dripping with charm, *perfect!* Bob thought, for a long weekend away to begin married life.

The wedding was a beautiful Scottish parade of colour. The men were dressed in traditional kilts, and the bride was radiant in classic white with a floral headdress and a smile that would shame the brightest of stars.

They both set off for their honeymoon, "Darling this has been a perfect day, thank you."

"Your worth every minute Mrs Jenkins."

"I like how that sounds, I think I'm going to enjoy my new name; Mrs Jenkins."

"I hope so, you will have it forever, you're not getting rid of me so easy, now."

Karen and Bob were laughing as they drove along the A 90.

"Bob, it's so lovely that your friend let you borrow his car, although I would not have minded going away in your, I mean our car."

"I know, that's what a best man is for; it's his wedding present to us."

"It's still very kind of him to loan you his car or should I say, his baby."

"Ah yes, baby MG, it has quite a ring to it."

"Yes, maybe we can name our first child after it."

"I'm not so sure our child would thank us for that, Karen." He said, laughing. "Although, it might make a great nickname."

"Well, if not our child, then definitely a pet." Karen added.

"It's getting late; I think I need to put my foot down a bit."

The sun was setting fast, and the light was fading with it; Bob began driving faster and faster, eager to arrive at his destination. Turning the corner, Bob hadn't noticed the stag standing in the road, majestic and proud.

"Look out Bob!" Karen screamed as they turned into the path of the deer.

Bob swerved the car from left to right, losing control and turned the car over, down the embankment and into a ditch. Karen was flung from the vehicle and landed in between an old metal fence and a fallen tree. She lay there unconscious and unaware of her injuries. Bob was still trapped inside the car, also out cold with a large laceration to his head. Both of them lay helpless and unaware.

"Hello, can you hear me? Hello!"

A voice from a passing motorist called out to Bob.

"Hello, sir, are you all, right?"

The passing driver scrambled down the embankment towards Bob, who lay there still.

"He's still alive! can you get help!" The voice said, calling up to another driver.

"There's a phone box down the road, I'll call for help then come right back." A woman replied.

"He's coming round; tell them it's urgent; there's a lot of blood. Also, I think there was someone else in the car, a woman! I can see a shoe. You're going to be OK my friend, What's your name?"

"My name is..., my name is Bob, is Karen all right?"

"Don't worry Bob, help is on its way, who's Karen? Stay with me Bob, who's Karen?"

"My..., my wi...."

Bob passed out again.

"Hello, do you need any help down there?" another voice called.

"Yes! Bob the driver says there was a lady called Karen with him, she's not in the car, I think it's his wife. He's unconscious again."

"Don't worry, we will look for Karen up here."

Bob couldn't be sure what time he awoke again; all he knew was that it was daytime, and he was in the hospital.

"Welcome Bob, it's good to have you with us, I thought we might lose you at one point. You have been in a very nasty crash and sustained quite a head injury, how are you feeling?"

Bob awoke to see a doctor dressed in a white coat standing in front of him; he had what looked like a clipboard in his hand.

"Where am I?"

"You're in the hospital, sir; you're going to make a full recovery, you're in great hands. You just need to rest."

Bob laid there, not wholly aware of what had happened, until a singular thought entered his head.

"Karen! Where's my wife Karen?" He kept calling.

"Don't worry, she's safe with us here as well. You can see her soon; you need to rest a while first. Maybe let some of the swellings go down around your head. You took a very hard bashing on your bonce."

Bob felt a little relief knowing she was here and safe, although he was unaware of her injuries.

A few days passed, and Bob began to feel stronger, all the time asking for his wife. "When can I see my wife?"

"We will take you to see her today, but there are a few things you need to know first."

"What? What is it? What's wrong?" Bob asked frantically.

"Well, Bob, she was flung clear of the car, a metal spike from a fence trapped her between it and an old fallen tree. I'm sorry to say the metal spike pierced her spine, the doctors had to operate a couple of times, it..., it appears she may never walk again. Otherwise, Karen will make a full recovery, she is awake now, lets get you up and ready, and I'll take you to her."

Bob nodded; he was too shocked to say anything; it was all he could do to take it all in.

The nurse took Bob's hand to comfort him; Bob could no longer hold his emotions back. "What have I done, it's all my fault! I'm so sorry Karen." The tears flooded out as Bob became very emotional.

"Sh! It's not your fault; it was a terrible accident. Karen will understand."

The nurse kept trying to console Bob's misery and disbelief at what he had done.

It would be a few weeks before Karen could come home from the hospital. In the meantime, Bob rented a small cottage and made it suitable for him and Karen.

Although Karen and Bob survived the terrible ordeal, life for them both could never be the same again. Neither could say they were not affected by it all, either mentally or emotionally.

"Karen, how are you feeling today? Are you happy to be going home today?"

"Yes, doctor, thank you so much for looking after Bob and me; I really do not know how we would have gotten through all of this without yours and your teams help. We are both very greatful."

"It's our pleasure, Karen. All we ask is that you do your best and continue with your physio; it's essential to your whole health. Will you do this for us and especially you and Bob?"

"Yes, doctor, I will do my best."

"Thank you, Karen. I know you may think as many do that life will not get better, but it will. Just keep doing what we've taught you."

Karen smiled.

"You owe it to yourself, Karen to live your life and make something of it. Go and enjoy your life with Bob."

The conversation with the doctor finished just as Bob arrived to take her home.

"Hello darling, your looking great, are you ready to come home?"

"Thank you, I am ready; take me home, Bob. I'm sure there will be plenty for me to organise. I can't wait to see the house."

Karen was already in her wheelchair with her bags packed and her good bye's said to the rest of her care team.

Bob and Karen left the hospital and headed home to their new life together; Karen never blamed Bob for the accident or held it against him.

Bob did all he could to care for Karen; some might say they had the perfect marriage.

Chapter Fourteen

George

Tom was back at his office examining evidence when George entered the room.

"Sir, I may have something for you, something I think could be a good lead."

Tom could see the excitement on his face and recognised the enthusiasm in his voice, which reminded him of himself many years ago.

"I take it your enquiry was successful; what have you got for me?"

"I spoke to a woman out the back, as you suggested. She told me both girls had a reputation and enjoyed a party."

George said the woman was reluctant to talk much to him but added, "she told me to question James. She then made her excuses and returned to work."

George added, "at this point, sir, I decided to come straight back here to report the lead to you. Was that the right thing to do, or should I have stayed and found out who James is?"

"Great work, constable; you did the right thing, coming back here. Thank you."

"George, how do you feel about coming over to help us more? It can only be as overtime; you'll still have to do your usual beat first, oh and the overtime is not likely to be paid."

"Well, sir, you certainly know how to pretty it up and sell it." He replied with a wry smile on his face.

"But", he continued, "I'd love to, sir; it sounds like a real opportunity, thanks."

"That's the spirit," Tom said, "We could use good coppers like you. When you're on your beat again, nip round to the club and see if you can find out who this James person is. Don't approach him. We don't want to spook him."

This news confirmed what Tom was thinking; the girls had gotten into something because of their naivety. All he had to do now was work out how and why it led to their deaths. The answers to these questions will lead to who is responsible for their deaths.

The next step would be to find James and determine what the girl's connection was to him.

George left almost immediately with a renewed spring in his step. He began to toy with the idea that one day he might also be a detective, perhaps even a famous one at that.

For now, though, it was to be business as usual, the day job first, then armature detective by night. Once more, he smiled to himself.

It wasn't long before Rabi arrived carrying two cups of tea, "I thought you might like this?" he said, placing one on the desk in front of Tom.

"Just what I need, thanks."

"Was that George I saw coming out of the room a few minutes ago?" Rabi seemed confused and perhaps a little downhearted; he thought he was the only constable helping Tom with his enquiries.

"Yes, the club we're interested in is on his beat. A woman who works at the club, gave George some information that might help us in our enquiries."

Tom then went on to tell him what George had told him, leaving out the bit about James. He was still playing his cards close to his chest.

"We're the only ones who know," he said, "the woman didn't offer her name, but it shouldn't be too hard to find out who, if we need to."

"What do we do now, sir?" Rabi's enthusiasm hadn't bothered Tom before, but now, for reasons he couldn't explain, it made him feel a little uneasy. Rabi was keen to keep helping as much as possible and be a big part of this investigation.

He pushed this thought aside, labelling it as enthusiasm like George. After all, he could see how exciting this could be for young coppers trying to make a name for themselves. Even he could see the potential for excitement. What better chance could they get, two murder victims, similar circumstances to a more significant case in London?

"Rabi", Tom called out, "I need you to do something essential for me. Are you up for the challenge?"

Rabi perked up and was up for a challenge; it seemed to bring in tea was a good plan.

Tom asked Rabi, "I'd like you to make a list of all known members of the club, make a note of connections to each other, jobs they did, and if any owed money." He also added. "This must be done without going to the club or speaking to known members; discretion is the key to this," he reminded Rabi, "no one must know what you're doing."

Rabi now felt that this was his moment to shine, his opportunity to show what kind of detective he could be.

Tom was all too aware of the effect this would have on Rabi, just as it will with George. He had used this man-management style before, which often brought exciting results.

He was now alone in the room, with just his thoughts to keep him company. He began to review the two cases in his mind.

A very disturbed individual committed the London murders; however, the bodies were ideally kept and preserved; this was important to Barry; he needed them this way for his pictures, which had helped to convict him.

The Edinburgh murders were similar, however, with marked differences. The girls were not well kept, they had bruises around their throats, and the handkerchiefs were placed differently on the girls here than those in London.

We also know the girls here were relatively poor until about two weeks before their deaths when they had been seen shopping for clothes and makeup. They were young and very naïve; neither understood what was happening until it was too late.

The key to this case must be the club; this was the horizon point and where all ends meet, which will now be the focus of the investigation.

It was later that George returned to the office to see Tom. He had been successful in finding out who James was. James was in his late twenties, slim, with brown hair and worked at the club as a porter. He would run errands for members that often consisted of bets on horses, dogs, and almost anything. James was a man of low moral standards. He repeatedly flashed large amounts of money around and was sometimes too familiar with club members.

He was well-liked by certain club members and trusted who seemed to wield some power over other staff working there. He was never put in charge by management and, at times, fell afoul of their scorn.

More importantly, James knew the two girls well; he would spend large amounts of his cash on them, treating them to clothes and promising them they could come to exclusive parties.

Tom instinctively knew where this was heading, and it wasn't good. One of these parties brought about the early demise of these two girls, and he wanted to know, who was there? And why it had appeared the girls were strangled?

Tom was highly pleased with the information gathered by George in his enquiries. Tom continually had a nagging question in his mind; *why make this look like one of his old cases?* It had to be more personal towards him. *But why?*

Chapter Fifteen

Paul Barry

Tina, Barry's final victim, lay perfectly still, almost serine in her appearance. Her beauty was stollen and cast aside by an evil monster, blissfully unaware that his time was up. Soon to be caught like a caged animal in just a few days.

Her long blond hair was clean, brushed and draped across her right shoulder and chest. Both arms crossed over her as if she were already placed into her coffin and final resting place. Barry was meticulous in his preparation of his victims. He wanted them to look perfect, which would mean preserving them to the very best of his abilities, washing them and placing them in neat, clean clothes. Making these preparations would often take Barry a long time; everything had to be correct.

As with his previous victim, Sarah, he had removed Tina's eyes, placed them in a small jar and carefully hid them under a loose floorboard directly under his bed. Barry later told the police that he couldn't stand the eyes of each girl watching him, even though they were already dead. "I must remove them!" he said; "they must not watch me". Barry was very disturbed at this thought.

Once Barry removed the eyes, he would carefully sow their eyelids closed using a blanket-style stitch. After Barry had completed this task, he carefully repainted new eyes onto the eyelids. He did this with the skill of an artist and a doctor's care.

One junior psychologist, hoping to make a name for himself, suggested that Barry's obsession was linked to an idea by Wilhelm Kuhne in 1857.

Wilhelm conducted what we may think is a rather macabre experiment today. He suggested that the eye works the same way as chemicals used in photography. To prove his theory, Wilhelm took a live albino rabbit and, after strapping it to the desk. He began a gruesome show that would prove his theory to the world, or so he would hope.

Wilhelm took the time to place the rabbit's head in just the right place, positioning it to face a window. Wilhelm did this while he covered the rabbit's eyes with a black cloth for fifteen minutes. At this point, the cover was removed, allowing the rabbit to only see the light at the window with bars running from top to bottom.

The rabbit was then immediately killed whilst it was looking at the window. The left eye was then removed and attached to a cork using pins, he opened it, and an optogram was made of the last image the rabbit had seen.

Rumours were floating around Scotland yard that in 1888, detectives were presented with the idea to help catch Jack the ripper. Many believed that murder victims' eyes could produce optograms of the murderer. The police never took up the idea at that time. However, it remained a possible idea after Wilhelm first made his optogram.

Barry never commented on this theory before going to his death. He rarely spoke to anyone about his obsession with women and his compulsion to pose them as he did.

Maybe another theory was that Barry felt remorse for his killings. Removing the eyes post-mortem would allow him to continue his most heinous crimes. One thing was sure, though, Barry was obsessed with another Victorian idea: Memento mori.

When Barry was finally caught, the police searched his home. They found numerous pictures of his victims, most carefully staged and posed after their death. Some photos were of the girls sitting, having tea or doing housework. In contrast, others sickeningly were posed in positions involving him.

Barry had developed the pictures himself to hide what he was doing from the eyes of the world. Perhaps after all the speculation, the phycologist was right; he was worried about Optograms.

Barry was a lonely man; he made his living doing odd jobs and kept away from people as much as possible. His father, who had long since passed away, was a harsh, cruel man who saw women as objects, there to cook, clean and produce children. This experience affected how Barry would also view women. Except that Barry had loved his mother and was very distressed that one day she just disappeared from his life when he was only ten years old. A body had never been found, although Barry's father did produce a poorly written letter. She said that she left for a new life and would one day return for Barry, a note that Barry had kept in his possession and would often ask for from the duty officer.

At first appearance, Barry looked like a kind, gentle person and was always very polite while awaiting his sentence. He never raised his voice and always tried to have simple conversations with officers as they brought him food and provisions.

It seemed he had almost accepted his future; made peace with all he had done and was now trying to make the most of what little time he had left on this earth.

His trial was very short, as the evidence the police had gathered was overwhelming. His pictures condemned him more loudly than any words spoken.

The key turned in the lock of Barry's cell; it was a cold November morning at 8 o'clock. The door opened, "ready?" the voice said. Barry just nodded in reply, his face sullen and drawn; he had not slept that night. He stepped forward and allowed the officers to handcuff his hands behind his back; his legs were shackled with a heavy chain connected to his cuffs.

The correctional officers led Barry away from his cell and up to the gallows; he paused for a moment; it was clear the reality of it all struck him with terror. "Don't worry," another guard said, standing next to him. "It will soon be over!"

Tom could see that Barry had urinated with fear, and for the first time, he looked ashamed. His legs became heavy as he lifted each one in turn to climb the steps leading to the noose.

The noose was placed around his neck whilst a clergy member muttered prayers on behalf of Barry's soul. A Silence fell upon the room briefly. The silence was broken by a creaking sound followed by a clunk as the floor fell away from Barry. His legs scrambled for the ground until the final moment, the last twitch signalling it was now all over. The room fell silent again; the only sound was the rope that continued to creak as it swung backwards and forwards for a short while.

Tom watched on in complete disbelief; he knew this would haunt him for the rest of his life. He could not see how much this affected him; however, he would not be quite the same. Capital punishment was not what he thought; how *could any modern civilisation be part of such a brutal way of punishment? How does a modern society punish a man or anyone who commits a heinous crime?* The thought troubled Tom for many years after this and would sometimes affect the way he did his job, often hoping for a better outcome than perhaps might be.

Chapter Sixteen

The phone call

Tom was conflicted in his thoughts; on the one hand, he liked Rabi; he had seemed uncomplicated and eager to help, Tom didn't have him pegged as a mole, but somehow this was how he felt. The question was, why? Why was Rabi now acting suspiciously, overcompensating in his speech towards him? Tom tried to put these thoughts to the back of his mind as he answered the call from Mary.

"Hello darling, how are you? This is a pleasant surprise!" he exclaimed. Tom was a little nervous, Mary rarely called him at work, and he instinctively knew something was not right. Mary told him about the reporters, with one being very persistent.

"I decided after you left, to take them all a cup of tea and a slice of cake. I played the dumb housewife card and made out I knew nothing at all." Mary felt she shouldn't keep any detail away from him. "One of the reporters didn't fall for it and although he left a few minutes after the others he said he wanted a different story. Then later that day a young boy brought a small bouquet of flowers round with a note to say sorry for his intrusion."

Mary had felt quite guilty at keeping the flowers; this had played on her mind for the last few days, and she thought it best to let Tom know. She wasn't flattered or anything like that, she loved Tom, and nothing could change how she felt. This was more about being open and letting him know she was in control. However, she had concerns and wanted to speak with Tom to calm her mind that everything else was going well.

Tom listened, not saying a word; it was only when his wife asked how things were shaping up there that he began to speak.

"I can't say too much about the case save that I'm now convinced the Scottish murders were not connected to the same killer as the ones in London." Mary was relieved to hear this and was convinced that Tom was not guilty of arresting the wrong man.

The thought of all this hadn't stopped her from worrying. It had played on her mind; with the newspapers saying all sorts of dreadful things, Mary knew he had a good moral compass and would find the answers needed to absolve him.

"Are you coming home soon?" she asked with hope. "No! it seems there is a connection, and somehow it still involves me; I need to stay and solve this case first, then I can come home; we're not out of the woods yet." Tom felt awful; he wanted to be there by her side as a family, but he knew he had to be here and see this through to the bitter end. This would mean a sacrifice; his reputation was at stake, and only he could protect it.

Changing the subject, Tom asked. "How Emily was doing?"

"she's ok, a little under the weather, she has a slight cough, nothing serious."

Mary didn't want to alarm him; after all, she thought it wasn't anything to be worried about; *a couple of days in bed will do the trick.* "Oh, one more thing, I was cleaning earlier, and I moved your jacket, a letter fell out of your pocket, its postmarked Edinburgh. Do you want me to open it and read it for you or send it on?"

Tom's heart sank; he knew he couldn't ask her to read it; after all, he had never really explained to Mary about Jane and her importance to him.

"No, it's ok, just pop it into the post, to the B&B, that is, not to the station; I may never get it otherwise." Now he was overcompensating like Rabi earlier; he just hoped Mary never noticed.

"I don't think it's important; it's handwritten, rather beautifully, I might add." Tom thought his wife was becoming more suspicious; what could he say that wouldn't ascend any more questions than he could answer? "I know," he replied, "some people have amazing handwriting skills, unlike me." He said, trying to manage a small laugh at the same time. Now I'm sounding more like Rabi by the minute, he thought; I will have to stop this going any further.

There was a knock on the door, "come in." Tom said at the same time as asking Mary to hold the line for a moment. Another P.C walked in and handed him a note saying, "we've just had a call; this message is urgent." Tom thanked him and began speaking with his wife once more "sorry darling, I have to go, something has just come up, and it's urgent, I'll phone you later, don't worry about the letter, just post it when you get a moment, I love you." He added, hoping this might soften the blow of leaving the conversation early. "Love you too!" Although it seemed a little strange, Mary replied that Tom rarely says that on the phone at work. She put it to the back of her mind, believing he must be strained and forgot where he was for a moment. Besides, she liked to hear him say that to her.

Tom, read the note handed to him; it was from George; it said to come as quick as he could to café Blanc, a small café off a side street from the club. The note went on to say; come alone.

This worried him; what was so urgent that he had to go straight away, and why alone? He put on his coat and hat, left the station, and headed off toward the café, his mind racing with questions and perhaps a minor concern for George's safety.

It wasn't long before he arrived; he saw George waiting at the back of the café facing the entrance. He didn't look happy; in fact, the opposite, he looked almost a little scared.

"What's up, George? Is everything all right? Are you ok? Tom tried to look more concerned for George than anxious. He noticed George was nursing a cup of coffee; "good call," he said, "I think I'll join you." As he sat down opposite him, he asked again, "are you ok?"

"I'm ok sir, thanks, but my contact, well I wish I could say the say for her. She had a terrible limp and when she turned, I could see a large, bruised eye; it looked awful and I think it's my fault."

"Why George, could it be our fault? Did you hurt her?"

"No of course not sir, but I think a man called James did because she had spoken to us earlier."

"I pleaded with her, but not wanting to say anything to me, she just walked away, so I persisted a bit more. This time a man whom I believe to be this James came out from behind the door, pushed me back, took hold of her arm and dragged her back inside, saying, she doesn't speak to coppers, and no one else will here either!" George added she looked scared, so he had decided to hang around for a while, hoping to catch a glimpse of her again or perhaps a chance to speak to someone else. "What happened next?" Tom asked, "did you see her again?" He could see that George was starting to calm down, although he was very concerned about his contact. "No, I didn't see her again; however, I did speak to a lad putting out some rubbish, and he confirmed James was still on the premises. And he added that no one is allowed to talk with the police, as accidents happen all the time and sometimes that means people get hurt."

Both Tom and George knew the back-room staff had been threatened, and whilst this was never good news, it confirmed that they were on the right track. Tom instinctively knew James would have a big part to play in all this; all he and George needed to do was work out why James was involved and what or who he was hiding.

"Come on, I'll buy you a pint; you look like you could do with it; we can chat about how we're going to nab James and get a conviction simultaneously." George liked the sound of that idea; he hadn't anyone to go home to; he lived on his own, just a cat and his thoughts for company.

George knew a pub further down the road and not too far from where they were staying. Tom knew that he could at least trust George with the bigger picture after that encounter.

It wasn't long before they arrived at the pub; they walked in through the double-stain glass doors. To the right of them, there was a traditional bar. Like most pubs, you can find up and down the country. On the left was a series of wooden panels, each separated by large mirrors curved at the top with a pendant light hanging from the centre of the panel with a medium-sized glass lamp holder. Beneath the mirrors were leather bench seats with round tables in front of them and a couple of chairs.

They walked up to the bar, where a barman was standing polishing a glass, trying to look busy but not too busy to serve. Looking at the array of beers on tap, Tom wasn't sure what to order; George said to the barman two MacLachlan's, please; Tom smiled and said to him, "you get a seat, and I'll bring them over."

Sitting there sipping their pints, they began strategising their next moves when George suddenly looked at Tom and said, "Brath Adair!" Tom looked confused, "It's an old Gaelic word meaning spies. We have a spy; someone must have warned the club and James; they knew we had spoken to someone there." This concerned George immensely; he had only told Tom and no one else. "Who could have known, sir?" he asked. Tom thought he knew but felt better not to say at this stage; he didn't want to cast suspicion on anyone until he knew.

"I believe you could be right; this case may go deeper than we think. Are you sure you want to be involved? It's ok to bow out now; it's not too late?" he wanted to allow George the opportunity to save his career and neck; he was growing fond of him, and he was good to have around.

"No, sir, I'm in it now; this case is under my skin, and I want to nail whoever murdered those girls and get James; I know he's in up to his eyeballs." George was happy to hear this. He, too, wanted the same goal but also to clear his name.

"That's the spirit; I think tomorrow afternoon we shall pay an official visit to the club and insist on speaking to this James and see what he has to say for himself." Tom wanted to check something with Rabi in the morning first before going to the club; he needed to know what Rabi had done, to whom, and what was said.

The following day could not come quick enough for Tom; he was up earlier and at the station before most of the day shift. Determined to find out more, he marched up to the chief's office and knocked on the door; without waiting for an answer, he went straight in. The chief wasn't happy at the intrusion and barked at Tom, asking who he thought he was barging in like this. Tom didn't care. He had justice on his side, and today he was going to find some answers.

"Why is Rabi spying for you?" he asked bluntly.

The chief tried denying it at first, then said, "This is my Nick, and no trumped-up London detective is coming here to tell me how to run a murder investigation. If you don't like how things are done here, you can go back to where you came from, now get out of my office, and don't come back till you have learnt some respect!" The chief was now getting red, and his voice began to echo down the corridor. Tom wasn't daunted by this; he knew he had struck a nerve and caught him out. He knew Rabi had been listening to his and George's conversation the other day and spilt the beans to the chief. The question is what he was now going to do about it.

He decided to let the dust settle and walk away; he left the office and headed down towards the main entrance hoping to meet Rabi on his way in. He was sure the eyes of every copper in earshot were now staring right at him. No one had ever challenged the chief like that before. Tom tried to remain calm as if nothing had happened.

Rabi came walking in, completely unaware of the excitement in the station and what had just happened. "Morning Rabi, glad I've bumped into you; I need your help straight away; come on, no time to lose." Rabi wasn't sure what was happening, and Tom wasn't giving him time to think; action was what was needed fast, furious, and immediate.

"What's up? Where are we going? Shouldn't I sign in first?" "Where's the car parked, Rabi? No time to waste." Rabi pulled out the keys and headed toward the car; Rabi was very confused about what was happening. Once in the car, Rabi asked again as to the destination. "We're going to the gentleman's club; you know the one; we need to get there fast but don't use the siren or the lights. Stealth is the name of this game." Rabi became very worried; he hadn't had a chance to brief the chief, which was Tom's plan all along. He was keeping the chief and Rabi apart, so they couldn't compare notes and use the information against him. He believed somehow the chief was now in on some sort of conspiracy.

They pulled up just a short way from the club, in a side street where they could see the back entrance. "What are we doing here sir?" "we're waiting for someone, you'll see, whilst I think about it, how are you getting on with the assignment I gave you."

Tom wanted to keep throwing him off balance, which Rabi knew but not why. "Pretty good actually, sir; I think I'm almost complete. I have over one hundred and fifty names; all I need to do is cross-reference any connections, and it's done." Rabi hoped this would please Tom enough to let him into his plan.

On the other hand, Tom was now very sure Rabi had blabbed to the chief about it all; there would have been no way he could have gotten all those names so quickly if the chief wasn't involved. "Well done, Rabi, we'll make a detective out of you yet. Do you have the list with you?" he asked positively, hoping to put Rabi at ease.

"No sir, I put it on your desk late last night, ready for you this morning, did you not see it when you went in?" "Sorry Rabi, I've not been to my office this morning this became a priority very late last night, so I thought it best to jump straight on it."

At that moment, George appeared behind them and got straight into the car with Tom and Rabi. "Morning, how is everyone today?" he asked; they both replied positively, except Rabi was still feeling a little left out of the loop.

"Have you seen anyone yet? You were here at seven this morning, weren't you?" Tom was eager to drop the net on Rabi. "Yes, sir, seven a.m. on the dot as requested last night, and yes, both persons of interest are here. They arrive just after me, going in almost immediately." "Excellent, well done." Tom was sure his mini sting would achieve so much on many levels.

Then the back door opened to the club, and out came the woman who had spoken to George two days earlier; she was sorting out the rubbish and still in distress, limping as she walked. They could clearly see she was also about to have a crafty cigarette break. Tom then asked out loud, "why did you tell the chief all our plans, Rabi? I specifically asked you not to say anything to anyone. How did you know this woman had spoken to George and given us a lead?"

Rabi was stunned into silence; he didn't know what to say; he wanted the ground to open and swallow him whole. Stumbling for words and feeling very uncomfortable, Neither George nor Tom would say a thing, letting him flounder as if a fish landed on the deck of a boat. Then before Rabi could mount a defence, if that were possible, Tom began to speak. "Because of you not following orders, this innocent lady who had helped us in our enquiry was beaten. Can you see her limping? she's covered in bruises and very frightened, her work colleagues won't talk to us now, making the job harder. Not to mention you put George, our colleague's life in danger, a fellow trusted officer. Tom had to stop and take a moment; he could feel himself getting more and more worked up. George never said a thing; he was almost as stunned as Rabi but delighted he was on the boss's side.

Rabi just looked down at the floor of the car, "what can I say, boss? I'm so sorry; I had no idea this was going to go this way." Rabi felt ashamed; he had allowed the chief to manipulate him into betraying Tom, a man he had once admired before turning against him. Tom shook his head in disapproval. "Why Rabi, why?" a few seconds passed before he answered Tom.

"Sir, the chief was breathing down my neck for an update; he made it sound like you were conspiring to save your own neck and career. He said if I didn't update him every day, I would not have a job, and if I did manage to keep it, I would stay in uniform forever. I'm sorry, sir, I should have trusted you."

A moment's silence fell in the car, and then Tom said, "I understand, but you did betray that woman and us, and you let yourself down." Before anyone else could say a word, the back door opened again; this time, they could all see James, standing there bold as brass and still treating the women poorly. They both went back inside, and the door was closed.

Tom looked at both George and Rabi and said, "right, we're on; here's the plan, George. You go round the back; give it five minutes, then knock on the door, walk straight in through the kitchen, and wait for us. Then after another five minutes, continue through the kitchens to us; if James tries to make a run for it, you can stop him there. Rabi, you're with me. We're going around the front to arrest James that way. I want him in cuffs and dragged out the front door as publicly as possible."

The other two saw that Tom meant business this morning; they were dismayed by everything. However, they both now wanted justice; they could see that everyone, in this case, had directly been affected by it, and someone had to pay the price.

They took up their positions, George in place around the back with Tom and Rabi about to walk in through the front door. "Take a deep breath Rabi, calm yourself, remember you're a police officer sworn to uphold the law. You'll do just fine don't worry."

Those words seemed to calm Rabi, who was now unsure what Tom thought of him as a person or a copper. "Follow my lead, constable," Tom said as they both walked in; they could see James talking to a guest and thought this would be the perfect moment to spring their trap. "James, I'm arresting you on suspicion of conspiring to pervert the course of justice, suspicion of causing actual bodily harm and assaulting a police officer...." Tom continued with the rest of the caution as Rabi began placing the cuffs. George soon came up behind them both from the kitchen, followed by one or two of the staff and one of the managers, "you can't do this here like this; this is a private member's only club, you can't be in here!" the manager began saying. Tom looked pleased with himself; he could see club members coming out to see all the commotion. "This should be enough to send a message to the staff, no one gets away with intimidation and violence." He retorted loud enough that not just Rabi and George could hear, but club members and staff.

Chapter Seventeen

Duddingston road

T hings were going well at the station; they brought James in through the back entrance like most suspects under arrest. They got as far as the booking desk when the chief appeared. "Richards, my office now!" He barked at Tom. Tom looked up and said," yes, sir, I'll be there immediately." He turned to Rabi and George, saying, "get him booked in, then get yourselves a cuppa, and I'll meet you in my office as soon as I've finished with his Lairdship."

They both smiled, agreed, and said under their voices, "Rather you than me." Tom looked back at them, smiled again, and said, "don't worry, I'm a big boy now." Then off he went, taking a slight detour before arriving at the chief's office.

He stood outside the chief's office, waited for a moment, straightened his tie, polished his shoes a little on the back of his trousers, and gave a firm knock, but this time he waited for a reply.

"Come in!" the voice bellowed from within. As soon as Tom entered the room, Tom saw that the chief was angry and somewhat frustrated with him. "Look here, Tom, what's going on with you, you barged into my office and accused me of interfering with your case you virtually kidnapped Rabi and force him and George into arresting someone at the club in front of all the members; what are you up to?"

"Yes sir, the club. The club you're a member of I believe along with some very influential people in business. Tell me, sir, is it the club members you worry about or your own membership that concerns you the most?" Tom wasn't in the mood to pussy foot around him anymore. "What makes you so sure I'm a member there?" "Well, I'm glad you asked that sir, it seems the list of members that I asked Rabi to compile, remember, the one you help with secretly? Well, having had a quick flick through it looks like a who's who of everybody that's important is a member, then I noticed your name in there sir, he did a very thorough job compiling that list, would you say so sir?"

On his way to see the chief, Tom had stopped off at his office to have a quick scan through the list before asking the desk sergeant to log it into evidence. He hadn't seen the chief's name; he just threw the idea together in the heat of the moment and decided to play a quick poker game with his career. It paid off; the chief began to calm down, he still wasn't happy, but he was caught on the hop and accidentally agreed he was a member.

"Did you mention it to anyone that we may have a suspect sir?" the chief was now feeling extremely uncomfortable. "Only our informant was badly injured not long after Rabi left your office yesterday. We confronted him this morning just before the arrest when we showed him the results of that conversation and explained that George was attacked because of loose talk and not only that, but it also meant the other staff members wouldn't talk to us because quite rightly they were scared. Now they know we will act swiftly to arrest anyone who stands in our way or attacks witnesses and especially those members of the Edinburgh constabulary. A result all round, wouldn't you say sir?" Tom stopped talking with bated breath, hoping the chief would agree.

"Hmm!" the chief muttered, "you know Tom, if you play with fire, you will get your fingers burnt. There are some powerful people in that club, and they don't care about either of us." Just then, there was a knock on the door. "Not now I'm busy," they knocked a second time, then, putting just their head round the door, said," It's really urgent sir it's the detective's wife on the phone, its about your daughter, sir!"

Tom looked very concerned, and the chief said, "but the call through to me, he can take it in here; I'll give you some space, Tom." A few moments later, the phone rang, and the chief left him to it. "I'll be back in a few minutes; take all the time you need." He said as he closed the door behind himself. Tom picked up the phone, "Hello, Mary? What's the matter? Is everything alright with Emily?" he said almost frantically.

Mary was in tears; "can't you come home?" She asked, "Emily's cough has got worse; the doctors are saying TB!" Mary could hardly control herself from crying. She continued, "Last night she had an elevated temperature and was feeling dizzy, this morning, when she coughed, there was blood on her handkerchief!" This wasn't what he needed to hear today, but he knew his wife and family needed him. However, he also had only a short time to hold James in custody, then he would have to charge him or release him, and the latter didn't appeal in the slightest.

Tom thought for a moment, trying to find a way to console his wife over the phone. Tom couldn't find the words he needed, all he could say was that he would be home as quickly as possible and that they now had a suspect in custody.

That sounds so feeble, he thought to himself. He needed a better plan than he already had, but how? he would need James to spill his guts as quickly as possible.

Tom knew his place was by his wife's side to help look after Emily; he was torn and at a critical stage of the investigation.

Tom was very concerned for his daughter enquiring further, "Is she awake? What medication are they giving her? What has the doctor said? Will she have to go to the hospital? The questions blurted out, one after the other, almost in a machine-gun style. He then stopped, realising that this was too much for Mary to take in all at once.

"Mary, darling, I really want to be there with you both." he paused for a moment, trying to find the right words. "The truth is, if I leave now, then our prime suspect who we have just arrested this morning could walk away, and we may never get another chance to arrest him. I will be back there with you both in forty-eight hours, I promise."

"Emily is asking for you!" she blurted out uncontrollably. Mary hadn't wanted to make him feel guilty; she was just trying to find the words to let him know it was difficult for her also. Mary was still distraught; she did understand the situation, although she didn't like it, and it didn't stop her from feeling down. Still, she knew he had a tough job to do.

Tom replied softly, "I love you, darling; tell Emily I love her too. I'll be home soon." He promised once more. He knew in his heart that it might not be possible to be home in forty-eight hours, but he thought to himself, at least he could try. He wasn't the sort of man to make promises he couldn't keep, but this one may prove the hardest one yet.

Mary told him that the doctors were letting Emily home. For now, however, she may have to go to a specialist hospital in Dartford called the Bow Arrow hospital. This worried both Tom and Mary. They had both heard rumours of only being able to see their daughter once a month. In some cases, not at all. It was a far distance for Mary to travel on her own, and on top of that, she had heard other parents say how they were not usually permitted to visit.

"Why are they only vaccinating school leavers at fourteen and not smaller children?" Mary was beginning to lash out at the still relatively young NHS system. Wishing that the new vaccine introduced only two years earlier was more widely available.

"It's no good, going down that road", Tom replied, "maybe one day that will happen; we have to be strong and hope for the best." Consoling Mary wasn't easy for him; he had tried his best, although interrogating criminals was more his comfort zone than tea and sympathy. At that moment, inspiration hit him, "what you need," he said in a kind, gentle manner, "is a cup of tea and perhaps something a little stronger; I still have some brandy in the cupboard." Tom hoped this would remind Mary of the two occasions she had said this to him and somehow bring a smile back to her. He longed to be there for his family and knew that under better circumstances, he would. Still, this time he had a duty to perform and a promise to the two young girls slain by a brutal killer.

With a heavy heart, he excused himself from his wife whilst trying to bring solace to his anxious and confused mind. Reminding his conscience that some sacrifices must be made for the greater good and being home right now would not catch a killer or make his daughter better. Although the conflict in his mind continued to nag at him, home is where his family needed him, by their side.

Tom left the room searching for his colleagues and devised a plan of action. This wasn't going to be easy, but then again, *few things ever are.* he thought to himself as he wandered down the corridor. It wasn't long before he met Rabi and George, "we have him all booked in and waiting in a cell; what's next, boss?" they asked in an eager manner and tone of voice. Both were now excited at the prospect of closing the case. Perhaps seeing their names listed in the papers may be a commendation. Their imaginations had begun to run away with them at all the possibilities this case could bring them. Neither of them had stopped thinking about the negative options that any of this could have. Also, neither had dared to ask how the chief was and what happened. Tom wasn't in the mood to tell them more about his home life, even if they had asked. His mind was now polarising and firmly focused on his prisoner and interviewing him.

Tom suggested to his team that a cup of tea was needed for them first. Tom explained that all the excitement so far could overwhelm them and detract from interviewing the suspect "also," he said, "it's good to let the prisoner stew for a while as it often makes them think we actually have more knowledge than we do."

He then instructed Rabi to fetch the pictures of the murdered girls along with lots of pages with typing and place them all into a manila-coloured folder. Rabi and George looked very confused at this request. Hence, Tom began to explain, "if we had pictures to show our prisoner and a thick-looking folder with lots of paper. It might help to convince James that we had a lot of evidence against him, and that people were talking to us now that he had been arrested."

Rabi and George liked this plan and secretly hoped they could store that idea for another time, perhaps when they make detective. Rabi did as instructed and collated 50 to 60 A4 pages of paper, with scribbled notes, lots of typing and pictures of the dead girls. He even threw in a rough sketch of where the bodies had been dumped. He felt proud of himself and was sure the plan would come to fruition. He also hoped inspector Richards would be proud of his ingenuity too.

George had been set to an altogether different task. He was to go back to the area around the club to observe who had been unnerved by this morning's arrest and perhaps ask a few more questions. Tom told him to only go to the club's back door and talk to the kitchen staff, waiters, and porters. He was to ask them about any strange comings and goings and by whom. Tom Said forcefully to George, "make sure you remind everyone that works there; we will keep them safe. And that anyone who gets in our way will be arrested and prosecuted no matter their position in life, Lord, Lady or Cook!"

Tom reminded George that more information on James was vital if we wanted to convict him of any wrongdoing. And catch not just the murderer but also the person or persons involved. "The more information, the bigger the picture, the better the complete truth will come out and only then can justice be delivered." Although George was a little nervous at returning to the club, his excitement was enough to quell his worries or concerns. After all, he knew he had justice on his side. Besides that, he had the great inspector Richards from Scotland yard teaching him how to be a detective and solve a terrible crime. Added to all this, he was also convinced that inspector Richards had stood up against the chief and hadn't been sent back to London.

It wasn't long before George arrived back at the club, and on approaching the back door, which opened to the large kitchen, a woman stepped out from where the large, galvanised bins stood. The woman screeched with shock; she hadn't expected anyone to be there and was clearly a little on edge after the events this morning. "Sorry, Lassi, I did not see you there." George said, hoping to calm her down. "it's o.k. I'm a police officer, one of the ones that came and arrested James earlier. Are you all right?" he asked in a calming manner, "you gave me a fright for a moment." The girl said as she began to walk back to the kitchen door.

George probed a little further by saying he was back just to reassure everyone that everything was going to be o.k. The girl paused for a moment and asked, "what will happen to him now?" "Well, for now, Lassi, he's sitting in a cell waiting for the inspector to question him. then with all the evidence we have, and let me tell you, I saw him with a thick file, it looks like he will be charged with all sorts of crimes and go down for a long time." George thought he also would apply some trickery regarding the file to help convince people to feel more relaxed and come forward with more information. The girl seemed more comfortable at that thought, although George could tell there was more going on in her head; she knew things but wasn't about to give up her secrets so quickly. "Did you know James well?" George asked, trying to coax her to talk more. "Not really," she replied. "I've seen him about, like everyone else here, although he has more to do with the members here than is appropriate for my liking. Also, many of the staff members fear him; he seems to have a hold over too many people." Not wanting to say anything more, she made her excuses and hurried away, trying not to look like she had been talking to him. He went to the kitchen door, which lay ajar, knocked, and stepped in. The kitchen was a hive of activity, the aroma and promise of a satisfying lunch for so many of the lucky, well-connected, not that he would get to taste or enjoy any of it. His stomach almost immediately began reminding him vigorously that he had missed breakfast this morning and still hadn't had a break to eat. Determined to press on and gather more information, he began trying to talk to any that didn't look too busy.

Whilst all this was going on, back at the station, Rabi began to look into Jame's background; it was then that he noticed that James had been in trouble with the police before. Many years ago, when he was a young boy at just thirteen. James had been linked, although never charged, with a grievous assault and extortion of money from a local shopkeeper. It was initially thought that James was only there by chance and that his uncle carried out the crime and was later charged and sentenced to eighteen months. Rabi took careful notes and decided to see if the shopkeeper was still in the area and, after a few calls, discovered that although the shopkeeper had retired and sold up, he still lived locally. So he took it upon himself to go and see him.

Rabi was met with little trouble on his journey. Although the shopkeeper was reluctant to talk, he could pry out some information. James's uncle was known for extorting protection money and would often be seen with James whilst making his rounds. The man went on to say how he had always felt James was being groomed to take over the business one day. He was convinced that's precisely what happened after the uncle was sentenced. This information excited Rabi, although he didn't want to let on and appear a complete novice. After thanking the man politely, just as Tom would have done whilst making careful notes. "Do you think James did take over?" he asked. "Definitely," he replied, saying that James was more vicious than his uncle and demanding, which is why he sold up and retired. He added that he had heard stories that James also supplied girls for parties at a cost. Plus drugs and illegal alcohol, there was nothing James didn't have a hand in.

"But of course," he added, "it's just here say, locally people won't say anything for fear of reprisal. He's a nasty, vicious man without any moral compass." Rabi knew the inspector would want to talk to him, but for now, Rabi just reassured the man and took his leave, wishing him well.

Rabi made his way back to the station, eager to tell Tom all that he had learned. Tom was sitting in his makeshift office, come murder room reviewing his notes when Rabi came bursting through the door. "Where have you been, Rabi?" Tom had been looking for him earlier and had become frustrated that Rabi had disappeared and hadn't informed him what he was up to. "I've been following a lead boss, a lead that I think you'll find very interesting." Rabi began to tell Tom all he had discovered, recalling his notes carefully, not wanting to leave any details out. Tom listened intently to all that Rabi had to tell. When he finished, he rebooked Rabi for disappearing without leave, then smiled and said, "Well done, great detective work, you've earned a seat in the interrogation room. I think it's time we went and had a little chat with James, don't you, Rabi?" Rabi Looked happy at this idea; he wasn't sure what to expect. However, he knew enough to sit and listen and let the inspector do his thing. Tom walked into the room, closely followed by Rabi. The room was silent, with Tom just looking through the thick file that had been carefully prepared by Rabi earlier. Rabi just sat and watched with intrigued, carefully keeping a close eye on James. Tom then looked up at James and asked, "Do you know what this is, James?" James just looked on in silence, waiting to see exactly what they had on him. Then Tom continued in a firm, very confident manner. "It's the file we have on you; it tells me all about your life, your uncle's business, if you can call it that and everything

you have been up to until now. It's a thick file, would you agree?"
James sat forward to pay more interest as Tom continued to talk.
"Back in the East end, I've seen lots of people like you, James, Young
men living in the shadow of a family member from an early age,
watching, learning, and sometimes getting to join in. Then when the
time is right, they step up. They only push harder and think they are
invincible, so they branch out, illegal alcohol, drugs, prostitution,
and so on." James wanted to interrupt Tom, but Tom would not let
him. He continued to tell James a familiar story.

"You're not very well liked, are you James?"

"Is anyone? in my line of work?" He replied.

"Hmm! you see, this file is full of witness statements against you."

Every now and then, Tom pulled a piece of paper out of his file,
saying they had at least two witness statements for each count of
wrongdoing. He would always show James the pictures of the dead,
mutilated girls. Then Tom Paused to let it all sink in before saying, "of
course, right now, I'm sure you will tell me that you didn't kill those
two innocent girls, but here's the thing, we know you are connected.
We also know you arrange a certain kind of party for people of
influence, and for the right money, you are happy to supply drugs
and young women. These two women specifically. Two young girls
of low means financially. Young girls with little knowledge of how
the world works, young girls who shiny objects and fashionable new
clothes can easily influence."

Tom Paused once more and pushed the pictures closer to James.
"Take a good look at them because unless we can make someone
else accountable for their deaths, then we will proceed with you. As
you can see, we already have enough to convict you of supplying
drugs, extorsion with menaces, evading taxes with illegal supply of
alcohol and prostitution. You will be going down for a very long
time, and if we add in the murders as well, then it's the noose for
you. So, this is your opportunity to tell us what really happened
to the girls and a chance to save your neck literally!" Tom stopped
speaking, and the room fell silent once more with Tom looking
at James; Rabi hadn't seen this side of Tom before and knew he
meant business. James looked up from the photos and insisted he
was innocent of their murders, "but you are guilty of all the rest,

aren't you, James? You've seen the proof. It's all here in black and white, witness statements, photos, and a whole catalogue of all your so-called business dealings. You can't deny any of this, but if you help me now, I can help you, I can protect you; however, if you don't, I can do nothing to save you. The jury will convict you, and you will hang, but you can stop this now, you're still going down for a long time, but there's always parole and a chance at a second chance in life. It's up to you. It's your choice, and you only have till I get back to make your decision." With that, Tom stood up and, signalling to Rabi to follow him, and they left the room. Rabi couldn't believe what he had just seen; he was expecting Tom to ask questions and grill James instead; he had just witnessed Tom bluff him with hearsay and very little proof if any. "Come on, Rabi, time for a cuppa, don't you think?" "Then we can see what George has come up with." Tom was happy to let James sit back in his cell to consider his position for quite a while, or at least till he could back up his previous statements.

George arrived at the canteen just after Tom and Rabi, who was excited to see him. "How did it go, George? we've just been interrogating our suspect; Tom was awesome." Rabi was perhaps a little too enthusiastic, but Tom just looked on and said, "it's o.k. Rabi let him speak." George began confirming Tom's assumptions regarding the parties, drugs, alcohol, and the girls.

"One or two of the kitchen staff have been happier to talk since the arrest this morning, but they are concerned for their jobs." Tom signalled that he knew and understood their situation; however, he still had a killer to catch, which wasn't going to be easy. George then said, "it was implied by one of the waiters that James's uncle was once in the employ of one of the members of the club." "We need to find out which member that is," Tom said, "and whilst we're at it we need to find out who was at the alleged party these two girls were attending. George, did the waiter say who he thought was the member of the club James' uncle worked for?" "No, he didn't say, sir however, it seemed clear that the club member was powerful and had a lot of connections including the police." "Rabi let's take another look at the member's list again and see if we can make a connection. George, I want you this time with me in the interrogation room; we're going to see if we can get James to let slip or better give them up."

They moved back to the room where James had been waiting for some time; Tom could see he was getting agitated and anxious.

"This is George, but of course, you have already met today, haven't you?" Tom was slightly antagonistic in his speech before moving on to what he wanted to talk about. At first, George just looked on in silence until Tom invited him to comment. "George, tell James where you have been today since his arrest."

"The club and it was most enlightening, sir."

"And tell him George what you learned regarding James's uncle."

"Well, that was very interesting sir, you see. It turns out that James's uncle once worked for an important club member there, and because of his position in the community and his powerful connections in the police, he will likely let James take the fall for the murders."

George had begun to enjoy his role in this scenario and was hoping not to mess things up; he could see Tom was in total control of the situation and was sure he could continue to help get the information they needed.

"So, you see James, it's not looking good for you is it, just to let you know we do have a list of all club members and yes, we know the chief here is a member of the club, so do you want to help us and save your life?" For the first time since they met James, he now looked very uncomfortable and nervous. "O.k. o.k. you must understand, I only supplied the girls, the drugs and alcohol for the party. I never attend them, and the girls usually get well paid and looked after." Tom could now feel that he was now making significant progress so probing.

Further, he asked, "How do you recruit the girls? And where do you find them?" James began to explain in detail how he would take referrals from his contacts on which girls might like to improve their situation and earn some extra money. He didn't expect the last two girls to be killed. "I don't know how they died or who killed them, but it had nothing to do with me!" James was now becoming very agitated and began to raise his voice. The thought of being hung now outweighed the worry of going to prison. James told how his uncle once worked for the club member; he had also served with him during the war. They needed this crucial information; Tom was now another step closer to finding out who this was; an army connection would be a great help. "This was why I was able to get an in at the club. My uncle did a few of the more unsavoury jobs, and I knew about this, so I used this information to expand my business; the club allows certain members to have private parties allegedly for business purposes, shall we say." Tom knew what was meant by this, but this left more questions, why were the girls killed? and why make it look like a copycat murder? Also, who Did move the girls, if James didn't? Finally, why arrange the bodies this way? He knew the answers were at the club and decided to charge James for the other crimes. This would buy him time to go home and visit his family and see if he could get a search warrant for the club, particularly the room where the parties took place.

Tom and George left the room, leaving James to contemplate his future behind bars. Tom went straight to the chief's office to explain.

"He's guilty, sir, of several offences and multiple accounts of each crime; however, as to murdering those two girls, of this he's innocent. I think though it may be possible to get him to lead us to who is." Tom knew this was his opportunity to take a couple of days off and go home to see his family. "Sir," Tom paused before asking about going home. "I need to go back home and see my family for a couple of days, especially as my daughter is very sick and may need to go into hospital. Also, there's a reporter asking questions about the original case similarities, and I would like to make a statement confirming that neither case is connected and that the original prosecution and conviction still hold true. Are you happy for me to do this?"

Tom thought it might be better to ask rather than assume everything would be all right. "Erm, are you sure this James isn't the murderer and are you sure we're looking for someone else not connected to your original case, it's your backside on the line Tom?" Tom was sure of himself and affirmed strongly that he was right, so he reassured the chief by saying, "I understand it's my reputation and the forces that's at risk. I would not make such a bold statement otherwise."

Tom hoped this might convince the chief all was going to be all right. However, the chief was not entirely convinced, so he pointed out that jobs were on the line, and it would be Tom's that would be first to go. Tom never replied to the chief. Instead, he just half-smiled, thanked him, and said he would return in a couple of days, then turned and, without asking for leave, he left the office, closing the door behind himself. Tom couldn't be entirely sure of the chief's reaction; however, Tom knew enough to know that the chief wasn't happy. Tom comforted himself with the knowledge that he had caught a dangerous criminal. Also, the arrest could lead to finding his victim's killer; added to this, he was looking forward to seeing his wife and daughter very soon, even though it was difficult circumstances.

Chapter Eighteen

Home

The journey home to Mary had seemed much quicker than his journey away from her, and although he knew it wasn't going to be easy, he didn't realise just how ill his daughter was and if she was even home or perhaps in hospital. Tom had not telephoned ahead to let them know he was coming; he thought it might be nice to surprise them both.

Tom clutched his suitcase in one hand, and his overcoat in the other as the taxi drove away, leaving Tom to let himself in, only to be greeted by his faithful dog. The house felt empty as he stood in the hallway; he called out, "darling, I'm home!" There was no answer; He walked further into the house, calling as he went hoping not to make Mary jump as she might be engrossed in something and may not have heard him the first time. Still no answer; after searching the rest of the house and backyard, he realised very quickly that Neither Mary nor their daughter was home and that something may be very wrong. Tom's mind began to race with fear at all possibilities; as Tom stood there trying to calm himself, there was a knock at the door. He opened the door, not knowing what to expect; his neighbour was in front of him, "Hello Tom, welcome home. I saw you arrive in the taxi and thought I'd give you a moment to get in before I knocked." Tom looked confused; he knew his neighbours were not the sort to knock out of the blue. "You look tired," his neighbour added, "can I come in and make you a cup of tea? I have news of Mary and your daughter." Tom smiled politely and stood to one side, letting the man in. "It's not all good news, I'm afraid, as I'm sure you know." Now walking through to the kitchen, his neighbour began explaining as he picked up the kettle. "Early this morning, an ambulance came to the house; Emily looked very sick, so she and Mary left in the ambulance for the local hospital. I asked if there was anything we could do, but Mary was insistent that they were alright and would probably be back home later today; she is a very calm and capable wife you have, but again you know that better than any of us." "What hospital were they taken to?" asked Tom, feeling very anxious. "I'm not sure; I think the local hospital down the road, I would say." Tom didn't wait any longer, "You can let yourself out," he shouted as he hurried out the front door, leaving his neighbour somewhat bemused and unsure what to do.

Arriving at the local hospital, Tom made his way to reception and inquired as to the whereabouts of his family. "What's the name sir," the receptionist asked.

Tom gave theirs and his details, explaining he had just made a rather long journey from Edenborough where he was working.

"If you take a seat, sir, someone will be with you very soon, I'm sure." The lady replied with a smile that gave nothing away; he knew he would have to comply and didn't want to make any fuss; Tom did think about saying he was a policeman, and it was very urgent but thought better of it, preferring to take a seat. Anyone watching this scene play out could tell you it was less than five minutes before anyone came, but for Tom, it had felt much longer. He wasn't sure if this meant good news or bad, he did know that he would have to dig deep and be strong. Tom stood as the doctor approached him; they shook hands with the doctor saying, "you must be inspector Richards, Mary's husband." He took some comfort in knowing that the doctor knew who he was and what he did for work. "I'll take you to your wife now; she and Emily are just through here. It's not good news. I'm sorry to say, your daughter has T.B, and we will have to transfer her to a more suitable hospital that can take better care of her."

"Will she be alright?"

"It's too early to say, she is very sick, and she has been coughing up a lot of blood, but at least you're here now; that will help." Tom didn't feel assured by this; he knew from his experience that the doctor had avoided answering the question entirely.

It wasn't long before Tom was led into a side room where Mary was sitting nursing a cup of tea with both hands, her head bowed low, praying in an undertone and sniffling with every other word. "I'll leave you two alone for a while, and I will be back in a few minutes." The doctor closed the door and left to check on his other patients. "Hello darling, I'm home like I said." Mary couldn't put down her tea quick enough, and after wiping away her tears, she stood up and threw her arms around Tom, squeezing him tight, sobbing her heart out.

Both just stood there, neither of them saying a word, only holding on to each other, each not daring to speak until Tom took her by the hand and led her to the two chairs by the window that looked out onto the car park at the back of the hospital. "I'm here now," he whispered to her. "Can you stay?" she asked him. He didn't know what to say; he knew that the investigation wasn't over and didn't want to choose between his family and the case he was working on. Instead of affirming his intention to stay to reassure her, he said, "for now," hoping this would be enough.

Tom knew that he would have to return to the investigation and Scotland; it wasn't enough to clear his name completely; he would have to arrest the person or persons responsible for the murders and prove the motive behind it all. This could not be done from home; it would have to be done in person, leaving his family behind to face this ordeal alone. This thought weighed heavily on Tom's mind. At one point, Tom almost convinced himself to stay behind; however, for now, he was back, and his support was needed.

The doctor returned, "There is a bed available at the Bow hospital in Dartford, and we have a vehicle to take her there now. I will take you both to see her, but I'm afraid you can't travel with her as it's the policy at Bow not to have visitors until they invite you. It's what is best for her now." Tom and Mary looked shocked. They had hoped that it would not come to this, or at least one of them could go. "The nurse will take you through, but you will have to put on a gown, gloves, and a mask to help stop passing on the infection to others as well as transmitting anything else to your daughter."

Emily looked very pale as they both approached her bedside; she hardly noticed they were there, all made worse by the protective gowns they had to wear. Barely able to talk and muster as much energy as she could, Emily smiled once she knew her daddy was home to see her. "Shh! Don't say anything, sweetie," Mary said consolingly, holding her hand "daddy has brought you something home with him; do you want to see it?" Emily smiled once more at the thought of something special from Scotland. "Here you go, sweetie," he said as he handed her a little teddy bear in traditional Scottish dress. "He even has a little set of bagpipes to play, just like the real thing; what do you want to call him?" Emily didn't answer; she was too weak and wasn't sure what to call him. "Robert the Bruce is a great Scottish name; he was once a king." He continued, "perhaps you could call him Robert or Bruce." Emily liked the suggestions and decided that Bruce the bear was rather fitting. It wasn't long before porters arrived to take Emily away, "Now be a good girl for Mummy and Daddy. Eat all your vegetables and get well soon, sweetie." Mary was trying hard not to cry and look brave for Emily's sake. She gently kissed her forehead, and they both waved and tried to smile as she was taken away.

The journey home for Tom and Mary was almost silent; neither knew what to say to comfort the other; words seemed too hollow. It was only once they both walked in through the front door of their house that Tom suggested a cup of tea, and trying to break the silence, he pulled out the small tin from his case and said, "I saw these and thought you might like them." The container held shortcakes, "there tasty and go very well with this cup of tea." He continued. Mary managed a small smile and said thank you, "do you think she will be all right?" she asked. "Of course, she will, she's strong like you, and she's in the best place. I know that means we can't visit, but it also means that she will get the best care." Tom wasn't sure he believed that statement. However, he had decided at that moment to be positive and confident to help Mary feel good about the situation. Inside, he was unsure of the outcome, which bothered him; like so many other things lately, this wasn't in his control; he knew he was powerless to change anything.

"Why didn't you say you were definitely coming home today?"

"I wanted it to be a nice surprise for you and Emily, and I didn't want you going to a lot of trouble to make something special for dinner as you have your hands full."

"I am glad you have come home, it is wonderful to see you."

"I thought we could have a simple fish and chip supper, what do you think?"

"I'm not sure I'm that hungry, but you must be starving?" Mary replied.

"Just a little bit," he said, "I'll nip round to the chippy in a moment after my cuppa,"

The rest of that evening felt strange, a silence they hadn't experienced since before Emily had been born. Tom would not have burdened Mary with the critical facts of his case except that she had asked him all about it, trying to show genuine interest and looking for the positives she desperately needed right now. Somehow this was helping them both, keeping their minds away from health concerns and focused on the bigger picture. Tom began to tell how the arrest was significant and although the murderer was still at large, James was essential; all he had to do was get him to confess to whom it was that moved the girls' bodies and why. He was sure their deaths happened at the club, and somebody was covering it up for someone of significant influence and power. Then, at that moment, Tom asked."Where's the letter please?"

"What letter?"

"The one I asked about when I was in Edinburgh."

"I posted it as you asked! Why?"

Tom wasn't sure if he was relieved to hear this or was now more worried in case Mary might have read it and not said anything. Moreover, he still had no idea what the letter said or if it was from Jane. Tom replied, "No Matter, I just thought if it were still here, I would take a look at it." He hoped his reply would not sound weird or worse, like he was covering something up. "I suppose you will have to go back soon," Mary asked. "Only with Emily in hospital and the case not closed, it makes sense you should return." This is not what Mary wanted, though she knew it was for the best; she didn't want him sitting around here getting under her feet when he could be doing something more constructive and worthwhile. Tom reluctantly replied, "Only if your sure you can cope without me; I can stay if you wish!" Trying not to make a big deal about it all and then added that he could stay a little longer, of course, they both knew in their hearts that the quicker he went back, the speedier he could solve the case and be back.

Mary knew that even though Tom was very concerned for her and Emily, he would have to return to Scotland to finish what had been started. It was for the best, so she continued to say how she would be all right here and if there were any changes, she would call him immediately.

The next day Tom had a call from Scotland; it was Rabi enquiring about his return plus updating him that James wanted to make a deal if he pled guilty to all charges. This improved Tom's attitude beyond expectation. He immediately consented to an agreement on the provision that James tell them everything, he wanted names, places, times, and dates, and if any detail, no matter how small, were left out, then the deal would be off the table. "I will be back tomorrow afternoon, Rabi; I will have to talk to the chief first and see what we can get, so no promises, just tell him I'm very interested to hear what he has to say first."

Rabi was now more excited than ever, he felt there was now a real chance of catching the killer, and it would be very soon. As a constable, a beat bobby before inspector Richard's arrival, he never dreamed he would be this close to catching a killer and on such a critical case like this. Rabi assured Tom he would not offer any deals, only to say that inspector Richards would return soon with an offer only if the information was credible and led to the arrest and conviction of the killer.

Tom was now more confident about catching the killer than he had been at any other time; he now had a theory regarding the events leading up to the girl's deaths. There were still unanswered questions, such as why make it look like an old case of his? Now with the proverbial bit between his teeth, he was more determined to find those answers. He was going to keep his promise to the two deceased girls and his family; he wasn't going to let any of them down, not if he could help it.

"Rabi, whilst you're on the phone, could you please ask George to call me? I have a job for him."

"Will do boss, I mean inspector Richards," Rabi replied in a rather cheeky fashion and feeling a little extra confidence. "Actually, sir, he has just walked into our, I mean your office; here he is." Rabi handed the phone to George, saying, "it's the governor; he has a special job for you." George took the phone from Rabi, "Hello sir, how's your daughter doing?" Tom was a little taken aback by the question and responded, "she's as well as can be expected under the circumstances; thank you for asking." George understood that it must be tough on Tom and his family right now and wanted to let him know that he was concerned and was happy to support him in any way he could. "What job would you like me to take care of, sir?" George added, trying to be more upbeat. "I need you to track down the service records for James's uncle and see who his commanding officer was. Don't tell anyone except me, not the chief or Rabi; remember, loose lips sink ships, George. Also, cross-reference the names for the club members to see if there is a match between any names for the regiment," George assured Tom that he would get right on to it and that he wouldn't tell anyone else. "Goodman." Tom replied, "I'm back tomorrow; please have all the information you can for me by then; I want to interview James immediately after I'm back."

Tom made his farewells and hung up the phone. Mary, still sitting next to him, could see her husband almost come to life before her eyes; it was at this moment she knew her previous conversation was the best course of action if only she could find a positive to keep her going.

Sometimes inspiration appears at the strangest of times; Mary began to tell Tom about the newspaperman who had questioned her previously and suggested that although he was only after a news story, he had seemed to at least have some integrity and initiative when tracking down information. Perhaps she thought out loud, "he might be of use in finding background information on those club members you just mentioned, maybe in exchange for an exclusive story."

Although Mary had thought this was a great idea, Tom was not so sure and immediately rebuffed the idea fearing leaks and damaging reputations with inaccuracies.

"Rumours and gossip released into the public domain are like emptying a bag of feathers on a windy day at the top of a hill. You can never truly capture them all back," Tom recalled what he believed to be an old Chinese proverb he had once heard, hoping it made sense and would detour Mary from this idea. Although Mary knew she should never interfere with Tom's case. She could not help thinking to herself that if the reporter were to be involved in some simple background checks, then at least it might help Tom solve the case sooner and give him other areas of investigation which may prove helpful.

Tom paused briefly to think about what Mary had just said, "What makes you think he could be trusted with all of this, and why would he not just put it in his newspaper for an easy life and a quick story?" Tom had begun to think more seriously about Mary's suggestion, but he still had strong reservations. He had never trusted the press before, and from experience, he knew they had only one objective; to sell newspapers, and nothing would typically be allowed to get in their way, not even the truth. Mary began to reply by saying,

"I share your concerns, darling; however, when all the other reporters stood outside pushing, shoving, and jostling with each other, trying to get me to tell them almost anything. I noticed this one reporter who had held back from the others and refrained from asking questions till all the others had gone. It was only then that he stepped forward and introduced himself to me." Tom listened intently to Mary and, with a great deal of concern, almost hoping to hear a good reason not to involve the reporter. When Mary had finished recalling the account, she, like Tom earlier, paused and waited to listen to what Tom would say in this regard. Mary was a little concerned as she had told him everything and not left out the part about the flowers sent to her by messenger and was hoping that Tom would not be jealous and dismiss her idea for that reason alone.

Against his better judgement, Tom agreed to at least meet with the reporter. He was a little surprised at Mary accepting flowers from a strange man, let alone him being a reporter; however, in the interest of settling the case as soon as possible, he was willing to meet up and at least talk with him.

Chapter Nineteen

Bernie

Since his encounter with Mary, Bernie had been hard at work following up other leads for his pet crusade. He had even commissioned a small survey on the streets of London asking people's opinions on the benefits and disadvantages of capital punishment.

Bernie was convinced that most people were in favour of life in prison and not a death sentence. Sure, there were always some who saw it the other way round. There will always be those favoured capital punishment as a threat or deterrent to others. However, most people considered it a barbaric sentence with too many possible mistakes.

Bernie decided he needed to be in his office at the newspaper to comb through any possible miscarriages of justice.

A telegram soon arrived for him, which read. Your *presence is required. Please meet me at my home address ASAP. Your discretion is needed. Inspector Richards.*

Tom had decided that he would not give away too much and hoped that this would be enough to intrigue Bernie into coming round quickly.

Bernie's first thought was a mixture of panic, followed quickly by intrigue. *What could the inspector want with him?* he thought to himself; *perhaps he knew about the flowers he had sent and was now about to make a big deal over it.*

Bernie was sure he had not done anything wrong or improper and was convinced that Mary would not have thought anything of the flowers. He re-read the telegramme this time and focused more clearly on the last few words; *Discretion was needed. If the inspector were to read into the flowers more than was intended and make a big deal over it, he would not have insisted on discretion.* This thought calmed Bernie down and excited his sense of mystery and intrigue.

It was not long before Bernie arrived at Tom and Mary's home. Pausing at the path, he took the time to ensure his appearance was proper, his shoes clean, and his tie straight. Bernie did not want to over-groom himself; after all, he was an investigative reporter, not a hack.

Tom was not sure what to expect initially from Bernie. So he had decided to keep things polite and civil; he did not want Bernie to jump to conclusions of his own and write something based on half-truths and conjecture. Bernie calmly walked up the path to the front door and, once there, rang the bell. Tom answered the door.

"Hello Bernie, please come in, would you like a cup of tea, Mary has the kettle on already and she may even have a piece of cake if we are really lucky," he said with a wry smile on his face, hoping to put Bernie at ease; after all Tom wanted more information from Bernie than he had wanted to give out in return. "Thank you for coming round so promptly," he added, trying hard to keep things polite.

Tom decided to probe into how Bernie was thinking, "are you working on any big stories at the moment?" Tom asked, "There are some ideas and possibilities ahead." Bernie was equally reticent, choosing to wait and see what this was all about before giving any information to Tom. From Mary's view, as she walked into where both Tom and Bernie were sitting, it seemed like a chess match between two grandmasters battling for the title. Tom had always liked chess and would often ask Mary to join him in a game in the quiet moments of the evening.

Mary smiled as she walked into the room, confident that Her Tom would be the victor in this great match of wits and determination. She placed the teapot, cups, milk and sugar on the table, saying, "shall I be mum, or perhaps I should leave you two gentlemen to talk whilst I carry on with my things?"

Tom could see the glint in her eyes as she said this. Whilst he had always thought Mary caring, dutiful and diligent around the home, he had always thought of her as his equal in life. He knew she was also playing a game, trying to appear as if she knew nothing of Tom's work. "Just to let you both know, the cake is about two days old; I have not had time to bake this week with everything that has been going on with Emily's health." Mary had perhaps given more away than she had initially intended, which Bernie had immediately picked up on. "Is Emily you're daughter?" He instantly replied.

"Yes, she's not well right now," Mary said, in a moment of self-pity, as she thought, looking back later.

"Emily has tuberculosis!"

"Where is she now?"

"Emily has been admitted to Bow arrow hospital."

"I am sorry, it must be challenging for you," Bernie replied. He had begun to show some empathy and dropped the chess-like countenance that he arrived with.

"I know the hospital well, it is in Dartford; the children's ward is lovely, they even have a small wooden roundabout that sits four little ones, and the doctors and nursing staff are excellent with them all. She will get really great care there; you will not have to worry about that at least." Bernie had hoped this might ease Mary's and Tom's worries.

"How do you know the hospital, Bernie?" Tom asked.

"I had visited the hospital several times over the years when it was used for another purpose. A while back, I was covering local people's life stories, especially those who do not have a voice to speak up about poor water supplies, housing and all those terrible illnesses that come about due to substandard living conditions."

Bernie could almost feel himself getting on his high horse again on this subject. It was clear to both Tom and Mary that he was a passionate man, especially about human rights. "Plus, he added, I covered the opening of the children's ward for this terrible illness. I felt proud to be part of that; it was a great day."

Tom felt at ease with the impassioned speech, not so much for his daughter's situation, although that had helped ease his mind a little. Of course, the main reason for his newfound confidence is that he knew Barnie was a man of principle, and if things were not right, nothing could silence him.

"Bernie," Tom said, "I need to share some information with you. it is extremely sensitive and cannot be spoken about to anyone verbally or in print because there is more at stake here than anyone may realise." Bernie looked at Tom in surprise; he knew that he had been invited round for a good reason, "why then are you talking to me?" Bernie inquired; he was unsure of his role in all of this and decided to ask more questions.

"Right now, Bernie, I need you to ask fewer questions and first agree that you will be honourable and abide by my rules of silence."

Tom had become very strict in his manner, almost school teacher in his style, his tone of voice changed to a more authoritative tone.

"I have a story for you, but before I can tell you anything, I need your promise." Bernie became a little nervous hearing this. However, he knew instinctively this could be big.

"Is this story going to be exclusive to me only?" Bernie asked almost excitedly but trying hard to not give himself away.

"Yes! you and you alone." Tom agreed. "However, in return, I need your help on a very sensitive matter. I need you to quietly do some background checks on a few people. I do not want any feathers ruffled at this stage or whispers of accusation before I am ready. Is this something you can do?"

Bernie smiled and agreed to the request but added, "I am not going to do anything illegal; I'm not that kind of reporter." Tom assured him that he did not want any accusations of illegal activity.

"This has to be done quietly, that's all, nothing illegal. The proof has to be obtained and documented for the case to proceed to court."

Tom had hoped this would be enough to assure Bernie of his good intentions to keep things level and straight in their relationship.

Bernie quickly agreed; he knew this would be good for him and the public, perhaps the real story he had been looking for all along. However, he was unsure how this would fit with the narrative he was already working on. What a great opportunity, he thought to himself, a chance to work with the great Inspector Richards of Scotland yard; no one else could boast that.

Tom told Bernie about the gentleman's club in Edinburgh.

"If you could call it that," he added.

Without giving away the details, he explained that the club members were highly secretive, as in so many they knew of here in London. He needed to know some of the background and connections of most, if not all, the members.

"I know it is a big ask of you, Bernie, but I am convinced the results will help catch a killer. That has to be a good result for everyone, especially the two girls' families."

Bernie listened intently to all that Tom had to say. He only interrupted to say, "So you think the killer is not the same one from your original case, given all the similarities involved?"

Tom looked Bernie in the eye and replied, "I am convinced we are dealing with a different killer. there are many similarities, I grant you, but there are enough differences to warrant my current thinking. Of course, this comes with a new line of questioning, such as, why make them look similar? and is someone targeting my cases to push a different agenda, such as the new anti-capital punishment movement I hear a lot about."

Tom knew enough about Bernie to understand that this was his pet project. At the moment, his agenda could have made him a suspect in all of this. "Does this mean you are pro-capital punishment then?" Bernie asked him.

"It's not my place to say; either way, my job is to uphold the law and catch those that do not. It is as simple as that. I can tell you, I was at Barry's hanging. It did leave a bad taste in my mouth; don't get me wrong. He was a sick man who did terrible things to girls that no man should ever have to think about, let alone investigate and look at their bodies."

Bernie backed away from the question and the subject. He could tell this was not the time or the place to question Tom further.

Bernie was sure that Tom had felt some sort of remorse for the outcome but still believed in right and wrong. He knew Tom as a good and upright man who stood for truth and honesty. This comforted him a great deal, but it also meant that he was not going to be shafted by Tom for the exclusive he so much wanted.

Tom handed Bernie a long list of names and underlined the most important characters to him.

"I would be grateful if you could make any connections between the members in the past or now. I am also especially interested in any, if at all, between this person and this name." Bernie had pointed to the name of Club president's name and to James, the man they had in custody.

Tom already knew there was and had asked George to look into this. Repetition or double-checking, Tom thought, was a great way to ensure he had all the facts, especially as he still was not convinced who he could trust.

Bernie agreed to make a start on the list and confirmed once more that he would not talk to another living soul about this. He liked the challenge of the list and thought that he might be able to run with side stories for some time after the main story had been broken to the world.

Tom, on the other hand, was more interested in the one story, the story of how and why these girls were killed, their story.

Whilst all this was happening, Mary had made an excuse to leave the room and telephoned the hospital to check on Emily. She missed her laugh around the house and the mimicking of their dog when the mail came through the door; it had only been a day, and it had already felt too long as far as she was concerned.

Tom had begun to walk Bernie to the door when Mary came back into the room; her eyes were bloodshot. Mary had been crying; even though she was trying to put a brave face on it all, Tom could see she was distraught.

Bernie left the house and headed back to the office, not his usual office but the real one where he was supposed to be when not chasing down a lead.

Before he arrived there, he had stopped off at the library to check out a who's who book on the landed gentry of Scotland and England. He thought this would be a great place to start; he also knew the connections in the army he could use to find out regiments and who might have served alongside each other. These things are often connected in many different ways.

"How is Emily today?" Tom asked as he smiled at Mary, hoping to illicit one back.

"There is no change. The hospital says Emily is stable. It is not fair; why will they not allow me to visit at least? She needs to know I am there for her." Mary became tearful again as Tom put his arm around her to comfort her.

"You heard what Bernie said; she is in the best place for her." Tom knew this would not be that comforting to his wife. Still, it was all he could think to say, even if it sounded as if it was only a platitude, rather than him believing what he had just said.

Mary knew Tom was trying to show his sensitive side and comfort her. She also understood that this was not his best skill; he was more at home with the business of catching killers and interrogating them. Strangely, it did help, mainly because they just sat on the sofa in prolonged silence. She cuddled up to him, with his arm around her, listening to each other breathe in synchronisation. As they sat there, the darkness began to fall around them, and the night drew in.

Tom knew, with a sinking feeling in his stomach, that he would soon have to leave Mary alone to her thoughts and travel back to Edinburgh. Mary also knew this in her heart, her mind frantically coming up with valid reasons to ask him to stay but never daring to voice them...

The following day, Tom woke Mary with a cup of tea and some lightly toasted crumpets, "morning, darling," he said in a soft voice, hoping not to startle her. "I have made you breakfast and thought you might like it in bed for a change."

This was not something Tom would generally have done. However, this morning, he had been up early and taken the dog for a walk to try and clear his head and perhaps find the right words to explain to Mary why he would have to go back today.

As Tom sat on the edge of the bed, sharing breakfast, Mary spoke, "you need to go back, don't you?"

Tom wanted to reply by saying no, he could stay a little longer, but he knew Mary was far more astute than that, so instead, he sighed softly and said, "yes." His body language said it all to her; she could see he did not want to go and was torn between the two worlds they now lived in.

"How much longer do you think it will be before you can close this case?" She asked him, trying so hard to be brave.

"Honestly," he sighed again, "I am not sure. If Bernie comes through for us and we can prove a connection between club members I might be able to push the man I have in custody to tell me more." Tom knew he could not give a definite time frame.

However, all his year's experience had given him almost a sixth sense. It was telling him he was close to unravelling all this and catching the person or persons responsible.

Mary understood this; she knew he could never be so precise; she only wanted an approximate time scale, something she could work with. Tom reached out to hold Mary's hand, leaned forward, and tenderly kissed her. Mary smiled and said, "I could get used to this every morning, when this is all over, I will expect this more often." She knew this was a one-off and that it was not Tom's style, but all the same, it was nice and a brief respite from their troubles.

"Maybe," he said, "when this is all over and Emily is feeling better, we should take a holiday, where would you like to go?" He continued, "or what about if...what if I decided to retire from the job, what do you think?"

Mary looked stunned; this was his life long before they met. Mary could not ask him to give all this up, even if the idea appealed to her. "Don't be silly," she replied, "what would you do? Take up golf or better still gardening?" she said in disbelief.

"I am serious," he said; Tom was not known for his spontaneity, he had always been careful, and thinking and planning was his way of life.

"Your serious, aren't you?" Mary could hardly believe what she was hearing.

"I am not sure how much more I have in me for this work," Tom said. "This case has taken a toll on me that I never expected. being away from home, working in Edinburgh, Emily getting sick, my place is here with you both, my family."

Mary was unsure if she should smile or cry at hearing about his thoughts and feelings.

"Why don't we wait until the case is over, when you have got a great result and conviction, then we can have the holiday and talk more about it then." Even though Mary wanted to say emphatically, "yes." She was not about to let the stress of all this compel him to make a decision that would change their lives forever, which would mean giving up something he had always loved doing and was good at.

They both agreed to talk about it at a later time, a time perhaps when things were more settled.

"I think Norfolk would be a nice place to visit. I hear there are many rivers for a spot of fishing and a picnic. Also, the beach is not too far for Emily; we can make sandcastles and go for a swim; it will be perfect for our family to relax,"

Mary suggested this as she had seen an advertisement to rent a caravan for a week in Holt, a quiet place to relax and unwind. Tom liked this idea; he had always wanted to try fishing.

Tom was unsure about the caravan; he would prefer a small cottage. However, he was not going to argue as Mary had painted the perfect picture in his mind to take back to Scotland.

The idea of a holiday altogether had seemed to perk them both up. Mary said she would see if she could contact the company that advertised the holiday and get a brochure. She now had a renewed focus, and there would be many things to do.

"The library would be a good place to get some information on where to go and what to see," she said. "When you return, I will have all the information we need to make it a great time."

Tom was pleased to see Mary feeling more positive and suggested that he leave for Scotland as soon as possible.

Chapter Twenty

Edinburgh

The commute back to Edinburgh had become less daunting to Tom; he knew what he could expect to see. He still felt a little uneasy as he had much work to do. Still, his purpose was clear and added to this, a holiday with his family in Norfolk was now his main focus and goal. All the other stuff was simply something he had to deal with to get to that point. He knew he had the skills, determination and experience to see this through. Besides, his gut instinct told him that it would not be long before he could return home, and at least this part would be over.

George was the first person he saw the morning he arrived, quickly followed by Rabi.

"Morning, Sir, and welcome back," George said with Rabi adding, "how is your family?" Neither of them wanted to be too direct in their questioning. Still, they were clearly concerned and asking out of genuine interest. So Tom replied, "Mary is well and keeping an eye on things back home; Emily not so good, but thanks for asking lads."

Both George and Rabi were shocked at their boss's slightly softer side. It was a side they had not been privileged to see previously, and it made them both feel that they were making headway in their relationship.

"We need to have a briefing this morning; why don't we grab a cuppa from the canteen and meet in our murder room in ten minutes?" adding, "bring all your notes; it is time we pushed this forward."

Tom was now more determined than ever. If this was going to be his last case, he would pull out every stop to go out on top. Nothing was going to get in his way. Nothing less than an excellent solid conviction to prove he was the good detective. Everyone had known him to be; his reputation needed to be intact when he retired.

He always kept his cards close to his chest regarding his personal life and career. Of course, Neither Rabi nor George knew that Tom was planning to retire; no one knew that except Mary, even if she did not believe it would happen. Only the people that needed to know knew.

Rabi and George almost felt Tom's return and renewed enthusiasm created an electric atmosphere. This renewed thought excited them both. Whilst Tom had been away, both of them had been chatting and working more closely with each and had created a close team. Sure, it was only the two of them; however, neither were now vying for the top spot like two lapdogs looking for approval from their owner. Now they were helping each other out. They knew almost instinctively that it was the case that was important, not them. Suppose they were lucky enough and did their jobs professionally and adequately. In that case, they both might receive a promotion, or at the least a commendation from the chief and who knows, one day they could be detectives, famous or otherwise.

As Tom had called them earlier, it was not long before the lads returned to the murder room. Though Tom had been busy in that small window of time, he had acquired a chalkboard and begun writing everything he knew about the case. On the wall next to the chalkboard, Tom had pinned the pictures of the two dead girls. Not the images after they died but the ones they had collected from an outside source, which were excellent, showing them both in happier times.

Tom did this to remind everyone that these two girls were young, happy girls with their whole lives ahead. That is how he felt they should be thought of, not the depraved way their bodies had been mutilated and discarded like meat in an abattoir.

"Great, you are back!" he exclaimed. "You can help me fill in the blanks; what do we know so far?" Although Tom had a good grasp of the situation, he knew it would be presumptuous to think that he had the complete picture and that his team also did. Tom lead the conversation by listing the following:

1. The Girl's bodies were moved from the place of the murders to the dumpsite found by us

2. Their bodies were intact except for the sexual activity and bruising

3. They were both recruited by James, who we have in custody, solely to attend certain types of parties

Tom Paused to ask George, "what was the link between James and the club?"

George replied, "it appears, sir, that he would frequent the club, not as a guest but more as a facilitator for some of the members, but not all of them, just a select few. We have also discovered the club has a function room, which the members use at times for special events."

Tom looked rather pleased with George, "you have been paying attention and working hard; well done," he said. "What else do we have, Rabi?" Tom asked.

Rabi replied quickly, "We know that the uncle of James, now deceased, served with..." Rabi paused for a moment, unsure if perhaps he should not say the name. "Go on, Rabi, we are safe in this room. Remember, this is only between us; his name will not be going on the board at this stage until we are more sure of his involvement."

Rabi felt assured by this and replied. "Lord Vincent, he is the club chairman and controls almost everything that goes on there."

Rabi was still nervous at saying his name, especially when George said, "He is good friends with the chief, who is also a member and an old family friend."

This thought worried everyone in the room. "Remember, lads," using this term again in an avuncular manner, "this conversation stays between us; I can't protect you if you talk to anyone about any of this." The lads half-smiled and agreed not to, they knew better by now, but the reminder was still worth its weight in gold.

"O.K., what else do we know?" Tom said in a perkier tone of voice, trying to redirect them back to the task. Rabi spoke up by saying, "he is married, sir, with one child, a boy, I believe, and his wife's father is also a lord." Suddenly Tom remembered the letter, "is her name Jane?" Tom asked. "Yes, sir, how did you know?" both George and Rabi asked almost simultaneously. Neither knew the connection with Tom from way back, and Tom was not going to give anything away, either in voice or body language; he was too long in the tooth to do that.

He would say that her family were English and had a flat in London. They had once needed special protection during the war years due to his work in the government. Tom hoped that this would be enough to allay any more questions.

"With these sort of connections, how should we proceed? I am sure we can't just ask them questions or point fingers, sir...can we?" George realised this was a sensitive point, although he knew questions would still need to be asked.

"Do not worry about that at this stage; when it comes to it, I should be the one to ask those questions to protect you both." Tom knew only he could interview a person of rank, and it would need kid gloves to do so until he had all the facts at his disposal. "Here is what we are going to do next. George, go back to the club and find out when that last event was there and see if you might find out who attended. Rabi, I want you to drive me back to my lodgings, there is something I need to pick up. Then we will go and see if we can introduce ourselves to lord Sexton and possibly his daughter Jane if she is there. First, though, I need to make a phone call."

George was not thrilled at the prospect of going back to the club. It felt to him that he was spending far too much time there. On the other hand, he did not want to disappoint Tom and let him down by asking if Rabi could go instead; that just seemed childish, unlike a would-be detective.

Tom wished George happy hunting and left the room, leaving Rabi and George to chat for a moment.

"How come Tom is going to see Jane already? Do you think they have met before?"

"I don't know if he has or not, it does seem to be a little strange, perhaps he was the officer giving protection to her father, who knows really?"

They both agreed it was unexpected, but Rabi was happy to be driving the inspector around again. He enjoyed that more than the other tasks he had been given, as it gave him a chance to ask questions about getting promoted to this job full-time.

"Well, as the inspector said, George, happy hunting at the club; if you get a chance to ask the chefs for a treat, they can sometimes be quite obliging."

"No chance of that, I'm sure; they never even offered me a cuppa when I was there the last time. Still, there is a first time for everything, I suppose." They laughed at that prospect as George left the room and on to his new assignment.

Rabi left the room also, carefully locking the door behind him, leaving a note on the door for Tom, which read, "I have gone to the car to warm it up; I will meet you out the front when you are ready." He thought this was the right thing to do rather than just wait around twiddling his thumbs.

Tom had gone to make a phone call back to London. He needed to know who the attending officer looked after Jane's father during the war. Tom also needed to see if he might be straying into sensitive territory by talking with Jane and possibly her father. The more information he had, the better when talking with the gentry, he thought to himself.

As Tom walked down the corridor, he came across the chief, "How are you, Tom?" he asked in his usual forthright manner.

"I'm alright, sir," he replied, trying to keep things civil and polite.

"How is your daughter's health?" as he asked this question, his face seemed to soften as if he understood what Tom was going through.

"She is not good, sir, she has been admitted to hospital, and they will not let us visit," He replied.

"That is not good for you or your wife's morale. Do you need more time back home till things get sorted? If you like, I can put someone else on the case; I know Bob helped you investigate in the past."

This was the last thing Tom wanted, to be forced to hand the case over to anyone else. However, if that were forced on him, he would rather it be someone like Bob. He thought to himself. "Thank you, sir, for your concern; I will bear that in mind; however, she is in the best place for her and Mary phones her every day, and at least this case keeps my mind busy." Tom tried hard not to let it look like he was not coping; after all, he was doing well and making excellent progress, but he was very aware of the connections to the chief. "All right, Tom, if you're sure, I will leave you to it then; when can I expect my next update?" Tom was keen to avoid that for as long as possible and so chose to say that for now, he needed to catch up with Rabi and George first plus see what has happened whilst he was away. Then on top of that, he had some leads to follow, then he might be in a position to give a more detailed progress report rather than assume some details and not be accurate. The chief seemed to have been plicated by this statement and asked if the end of the week would be a better time to catch up on everything. Tom agreed by saying simply, "Yes, quite possibly, sir." He did not want to be too definite about the day or time as it all depended on what happened over the next few days.

They both made their farewells and continued with their tasks at hand. All the time, Tom wondered if the chief was involved. Of course, if he did update him on the exact line of enquiry, would he then leak this information to lord Vincent? Questions that could not be answered immediately? Now, he needed more time.

Tom called London; he knew he could not go through the usual channels, so he decided to speak to a retired colleague, who proved to be very helpful. Jane's father, lord Sexton, was from good reliable stock. He served his country with dignity and honour. He was rumoured to have been instrumental in many successful covert operations during the war. Which had been reported to have saved thousands of lives. This was good news for Tom; he knew lord Sexton could be trusted and was almost certainly discrete. This gave him confidence, especially as he was about to go and get reacquainted with Jane; he wasn't sure what to expect, good, bad or indifferent.

He returned to his murder room, expecting to find Rabi and read the note he had left pinned to the door; Tom tried the handle and found it was locked. *Rabi was displaying a good deal of caution*, he thought to himself. It was not long before he caught up with Rabi outside, and together they headed to the B & B Tom had been staying in. Not long before they arrived, Tom turned to Rabi and said, "I will only be a minute or two if you don't mind waiting here." Rabi was unsure what was happening but was happy to wait in the car. Tom left Rabi and went inside to see if Hannah, Han as she liked to be called, had received any mail for him and let her know that he was back.

"Hello, inspector Richards," came a voice behind the door, "I see you're back with us again; how is your family?" Han was clearly very excited to see Tom again and offered him his room back, "it is your room and no one else," she said with a large welcoming smile.

"Thank you, Mrs...I mean Han, has there been any mail for me, please?" Tom asked, almost relieved to be back here again. Han replied with a smile, knowing Tom did not find it easy to be less formal with people.

"Yes, I have a letter for you just here; it looks like it came from London, although you can tell that there is also a second letter within it." Han continued, "May I have the stamp when you finish with the letter?" She asked, "Only the stamp looks an interesting one in blue with a castle on it and what a wonderful likeness of the Queen also." Tom agreed; not wanting to stay chatting, he hoped he might be able to leave at this point. However, Han continued, "What do you think of her, the Queen? That is, do you think she will be a good Queen? I wonder how long she will reign; what do you think?"

Tom did not want to be engaged in conversation any longer and simply replied. "She is young, so hopefully, she will have a long while yet to lead the country." Tom decided this would be an excellent point to stop the conversation. He told the landlady that he had a car waiting outside and that he had some important business to take care of.

Han understood and replied, "of course, you are a very busy man and have an important job to do; I will not keep you any longer; I will see you tonight, I am sure." Tom smiled and simply replied, "thank you." He quickly made his way up to his room to read his letter alone, opening it as he went.

Han, the landlady, was correct; of course, two letters were inside. The first was from Mary, his wife; he recognised the handwriting immediately. Tom wanted to read it even though he knew he had already seen her after the letter had been sent. But Tom also knew he had not got much time so instead, he chose to open the letter from Jane. He sat down on the edge of his bed and carefully opened up the letter, and began to read it in an undertone to himself.

"*Dear Tom, I hope this letter is well received and that you and your family are keeping safe and well. I know it has been a long time since we last spoke and our lives have gone off in two very different directions than perhaps we may have first thought.*"

Tom's heart was pounding hard with a mixture of emotions, with the thought of anticipation of what Jane would say. This could bring anxiety if it were a letter declaring inappropriate intentions. *How would Mary feel if she watched him right now as he opened the letter and sat down to read it? If I were Mary,* he thought, *what would I be thinking? How does this situation look?* Tom felt more furtive, a feeling he had never thought possible for him.

Tom read the entirety of the letter, looked up and smiled to himself, "what a fool? How could I have been so stupid?" Tom began berating himself, not in a wrong way but more in the form of giving himself a kick up the pants. His mood lifted as he felt less like he was acting illicitly. Tom knew at that moment his next step was to visit the house of lord Sexton to discuss the contents of Jane's letter and, of course, learn when would be an appropriate time to call on Jane herself. Tom stood up and collected his things; he quickly and calmly walked downstairs to where Rabi had been waiting patiently in the car.

"Sorry, Rabi. I had not meant to take so long, my landlady wanted to chat; still, it is a bright new day and I think it is time we visit a certain lord Sexton's house. Do you know where he lives? I have his address if you need it." Tom's mood was lifting and becoming more positive by the minute. "That's all right Sir, your the guv, and yes I know the way thank you."

Rabi had responded to Tom's lighter mood with a bit of cheekiness of his own.

Chapter Twenty-One

Jane 1955

Jane had woken up early that morning in a reflective mood; she had not been able to sleep much that night and knew why. *Should I write to Tom?* she had asked herself repeatedly. *It would be lovely to hear from him and perhaps meet again.* Jane was aware of the risks and consequences of getting in contact with Tom after all these years. Not just for her but also others, and this included how Tom and his family would feel. Jane knew he had married some years after their heart-breaking departure at the train station and that he and his wife now had a little girl. She did not want to cause any problems or divisions; however, burning inside her was the need to write to him and explain. Jane continued thinking. Hoping to convince herself that it would be fine if she could explain her feelings and the situation she now found herself coping with.

Sitting at her desk, Jane picked up her pen, ready to inscribe her innermost thoughts on paper; she had so much to say but finding the right words proved harder than she had thought initially. Jane decided that she would get dressed and have breakfast first in the hope that the extra time would help her think; she knew that her words would need to be carefully chosen if her letter was successful.

A few minutes later, lord Sexton, Jane's father, called her on the telephone, "Morning Darling, have you had time yet to write to Tom?" he inquired. Jane replied, "I am just having breakfast now and was about to start very soon, but it feels wrong and disloyal." Jane did not want to write the letter. However, she knew that she had not got many choices. Lord Sexton quickly added, "from what you have said in the past, Jane, about his character, he is the person we need to help save the family name." Jane let out a small sigh; she knew it was the only way; it did not feel entirely right involving Tom. However, she knew that she and her father could rely on him to do the right thing. "Don't worry, Daddy, I will write it today and ask for his help; I am sure he will understand."

Jane knew that she could not put off writing any longer; her mind was still racing with guilt at what she was about to do. Jane hung up the phone and walked into her study. Her desk beckoned her to her fate and a road she could not return from easily. The pen in her hand felt heavier than usual as she forced herself to write.

Dear Tom, I hope this letter is well received and that you and your family are keeping safe and well. I know it has been a long time since we last spoke, and our lives have gone off in two very different directions than perhaps we may have first thought. I have often fondly remembered the times we had together. How our friendship had seemed so deep-seated and sure, I especially remember the support we both gave each other during the war's difficult and dark days. Sometimes I muse with the thoughts of what might have happened if things had been different. Perhaps this is the case for many people who were thrown together quite unexpectedly during those years. I do hope with all my heart that you and your family are enjoying life to the full. With this in mind, I hope you can forgive me for intruding into your family's life utilising this letter. However, my father and I need your help most urgently. I know you are possibly the only person we can rely upon for discretion. And to help resolve what is now proving to be both a delicate and challenging situation. I appreciate that this may seem inappropriate and perhaps unorthodox; however, my intentions are honest and pure. I would not want to cause any trouble or difficulties for you or your family. I cannot say any more in this letter for fear it may be misconstrued and used in a way that does not befit a man of your impeccable standing. I would appreciate it if you would return this correspondence to me or my father using the return address written over the leaf with an acknowledgement and assurance of help. My father and I will be eternally in your and your family's debt.

kindest regards,
Jane.
P.S. Both my father and I fully understand if you would prefer not to correspond or help regarding our situation.

Jane read the letter repeatedly, continuously making changes not to seem overly dramatic or maudlin. She had wanted to strike the right tone and balance. It was essential to her to impress on Tom just how much they needed his help with the problematic situation they found themselves dealing with. The clock in the study had long since chimed past the hour of one p.m before Jane felt happy with her letter. Due to circumstances, it still bothered her that she was forced into writing it and asking for help; this was something she was not used to in recent years. However, she continued to remind herself that this was for the greater good and not for her. Jane sealed the envelope and carefully added Tom's address which her father had acquired through some of his old contacts. If nothing else in all this sorry mess, she was grateful that her father still maintained his relationships and connections from the war years. She had always known he was well connected. However, her father never spoke of his work. Nor did he say about the unimaginable situations and decisions he had been involved in. All to protect the country from the ravages of Hitler. This would comfort Jane in the coming days. Knowing his fortitude, strength, and moral uprightness would see them through the "darkest hours" ahead, as Churchill had once quoted so famously.

Jane was now renewed in her confidence. Jane drove to the post office and purchased the stamp to ensure the letter was posted, not leaving anything to chance. It was not quite the hopes of the nation or the declaration of peace, she told herself; however, it felt the same to her.

Jane felt a modicum of relief after she had posted the letter. She knew now that whatever was to happen would be without her control; she had set the wheels in motion, to which there was no going back. Jane drove home not knowing what to expect, only stopping to telephone her father to tell him it was now done; the letter had been posted. "Are you sure we have done the right thing?"

She asked him, looking for comfort, "of course we have, you may have written the letter, but we have done this together; it will be a bumpy road for a while, but you will see, the sun will shine, my darling again." Jane felt comfort from his words, knowing he was always right.

Several days had passed since Jane had sent her letter, and she knew that Tom might not reply immediately. However, she had not counted on no reply; after all, she was sure the letter was not upsetting or controversial in any way. "How could it be?" This thought kept pounding her mind like the waves of the North sea being driven by the winter winds. She had often experienced this whilst on the coast walking, the relentless taunting this caused her and every time left a sinking feeling in the pit of her stomach. She was unsure what her next move should be; should she telephone him at Scotland yard or perhaps at his home? What if Mary was to answer the phone? What would she say? Jane could understand if this was anything like her father faced during the war. He had so many late nights in his office that sometimes she could see that he had not slept in days, yet he still found the strength to carry on while putting on a brave face for her and others around him. Jane knew that since her mother died when she was only a tiny girl, her father often had no one to talk to to share his concerns. He prefered not to burden Jane. On the other hand, she had always believed that she could cope with knowing but was sometimes pleased that he had not, especially when she could see the toll it had taken on him.

The next few days seemed to pass by slowly, with every hour dragging. Sometimes, she amused herself with the notion that Tom would charge in as if on his white horse and dress like a night in shining armour, a vision she had always had of her father as a little girl. Then on other occasions, it was despair that he would never reply. Perhaps he had all but forgotten her. Now her fate was beckoning her and her family to a bitter conclusion. At this point, Jane decided that trying to contact Tom again was not the best thing to do or the right thing; she could go and see her father and spend some time with him. He was retired, getting on in age, due to arthritis and possibly a little Gout was sometimes unsteady on his feet. She thought this would give her the best excuse to go and spend some time with him.

That night at dinner, Jane spoke with lord Vincent, her husband and suggested the idea of going to stay with her father by saying.

"I spoke with daddy earlier today; he is not feeling too well. I think it is his usual trouble." Jane paused for a moment, not wanting to make it look too apparent what she was up to and at the same time trying to find the right way to suggest that she should go on her own to see him for a few days.

Lord Vincent did not seem overly interested in the conversation or concerned at what Jane had just told him, so Jane then added, "I should go and stay for a few days, just till he is feeling a bit chirpier, what do you think?" Lord Vincent still did not seem to be too bothered and replied, "of course dear, whatever you think is best!"

Jane knew his mind was elsewhere, work perhaps or the freedom it would give him to spend more time at that retched club that she so despised. Jane believes it to be a bastille of male dominance and misogynistic attitudes. Jane also knew that her father was a member of the same club. However, it was different for him. Lord Sexton was a member of a couple of clubs. The club is where he did business and often pushed and persuaded other members to contribute to his many worthy causes. Many of which was Jane's, except she had talked her father into supporting them on her behalf.

Jane could never know what her husband was thinking. Lord Vincent had always seemed indifferent to Jane's suggestions regarding her father. He rarely seemed interested in dinner conversation unless it was about him or something he was interested in. Her father's health or ideas on how he should conduct business or run his life would never be a topic for conversation.

Then quite unexpectedly, lord Vincent suggested, "After dinner perhaps I should give him a call, we rarely see him at the club nowadays." This was not what Jane had wanted at all; she did not want her husband interfering; however, what could she say in reply if she said otherwise to him? He might become suspicious and perhaps go even further by suggesting he come along also to visit. Jane tried hard not to panic at this thought. Instead, she replied, "You are so busy at the moment, I can tell, you look tired, why not let me run you a bath after dinner then call daddy in the morning, anyway when I spoke earlier with him he said he was having an early night as he has not been sleeping too well."

Jane stopped speaking at this point, not wanting to over-egg the cake. Perhaps it was her overactive imagination causing her to read more into the conversation than was there. Her husband reluctantly agreed, although somehow she could tell he knew she was up to something.

The next day could not come too quickly. Like so many nights before, Jane had not suitably slept. She was sure that after last night's conversation, her husband was suspicious of what she was trying to do. Jane tried to continue her usual routine. She came downstairs and into the hallway, and whilst passing her husband's study, she could hear he was on the telephone. Jane had hoped that her husband may have decided not to phone or, better still, entirely forgotten about calling him. However, before hanging up the phone, Jane could hear him wishing lord Sexton well. Jane grew very concerned. She had not had a chance to warn her father that her husband might call to inquire about his health nor that she would be coming over to stay for a few days under the guise of helping to regain his health.

Jane decided to play it cool and not say anything to arouse suspicion. Her husband left his study and passed Jane in the hall; as he left the house, he called out to her, saying, "let me know you have arrived at your father's house safely, and let me know when you are coming home." He smiled as he closed the front door, left and headed to work. Jane was unsure what to make of this turn of events and felt quite uneasy. Determined not to be put off, she packed a few things into a case and left the house not long after her husband, deciding that the sooner she was at her father's house, the better she would be.

After arriving at her family home, she rushed in to find her father, "Daddy!" she called out whilst going straight to his study, expecting to see him there. "Daddy!" she called out again; upon discovering he was not there, she eventually found him in the greenhouse attending to his orchids. "What is up?" He asked, "you look flushed," he continued, "take a moment to catch your breath, my dear." "It's

Reginald; he called you this morning!" she blurted out. "Yes, he did, but don't worry, I guessed what was happening. He has never called me to inquire about my health or well-being before. I decided to play along to see what happened; you know Jane, I was in the secret service. We have an instinct about these things. That coupled with top-notch training, well, let's say, there is a good reason our side won the war."

He smiled and said, "come on, let's go and have a lovely cup of tea, the other reason we won the war." Jane hugged her father, knowing that the plan was in safe hands, well with him at least, she thought, especially as Tom had yet to contact her still if he ever would.

They sat together in the conservatory, enjoying the morning sunshine pouring through the glass panes. However, it was still icy outside; the crisp, bright new day brought not just the sunlight but also an optimism to Jane that she had not felt in a long time. She was not sure why but sitting there with her father sipping tea, somehow she knew that it would not be too long before things would change for the better.

"Daddy, have you heard anything from Tom yet? only, I have not heard a word, not a letter or call to say if he can help us or not." Jane asked.

"One thing I have learned," her father said. "Is that patience was most often the hardest quality when you are desperate for news, yet more often than not, it would bring about the best results."

Jane knew that she had lacked patience growing up. Although she had heard her father tell her this many times over the years. It was still often challenging for her to put it into practice even now as an adult. Alas, though, she would have to resolve to do so for everyone's benefit once more, and who knows, maybe for one more time, things will work out right for everyone, she thought.

"I suppose I could make a few calls to check his status. He might be away from work on leave. That would be a perfectly acceptable reason for not reading the letter and replying." Lord Sexton suggested to try and comfort Jane further. "I will go to my study and see what I can do; I will not be too long; you stay here and enjoy the rest of your tea. Then hopefully, when I return, I will have some good news for us both and if not, at least we will know where we both stand."

Jane could only manage a small smile based on fear of what might happen if it were not good news. However, it was a plan, and that would have to be enough for now for her. Lord Sexton went off to his study to make his call when the front doorbell sounded. "That is curious," he thought to himself; after all, he was not expecting any visitors today. Lord Sexton walked to the front door with his walking stick in hand, arriving only a few moments after his butler had answered the door. He stood to one side within hearing distance but out of sight of everyone else. "Good morning, sirs. How may I help you?" The butler asked.

Chapter Twenty-Two

Tom and Jane meet again

R abi drove the car through the open gates and followed the gravelled driveway as it twisted from right to left. As it did, they passed through a small wooded area, which opened up to a view that surprised even Tom. There, in front of Tom, stood a house larger than was ever imaginable for one family. There were four large steps leading up to an area surrounded by a formal-looking garden, then six more steps up to the front door. "Does one family really live here?" Tom asked Rabi. "Where I live, there would be at least six or seven large families that lived here." Tom was taken aback and could not believe that his old friend Jane and her family lived here, surrounded by such luxury and beauty. Yet, with all of this, he knew Jane to be a caring and down-to-earth person. He was almost glad he had not asked Jane to marry him and stay with him in London; how could he have ever hoped to provide anything like this or even come close to it?

Rabi laughed and replied, "I know, sir, it does not seem right that people can have so much when others have so little. I just hope that one day we will all be more equal and no child would go hungry." Rabi had revealed so much about the way he thinks and feels to Tom by this statement, Tom knew Rabi was a man of the people, but this showed a more profound, caring side to him that Tom liked. "Have you been here before Rabi?" Tom asked as they were getting out of the car. "No sir, but I believe a number of years ago there was an incident regarding trespassing here; lord Sexton did not want to prosecute the man in question in the hope of fostering good relationships with the locals, one of my colleagues came and took a statement but that was all." Tom was not sure how this would play out, so he wanted to prepare Rabi a little first. "It will be best to let me do all the talking," Tom suggested. "I will introduce myself, then you and then ask if it may be possible to see lord Sexton today, immediately, I find it best to catch people unaware sometimes." Rabi replied simply by saying, "yes."

"Oh, and one more thing whatever happens here stays between you and me, discretion is paramount with these people, at least till we know what is going on and we have the bigger picture." "That makes sense sir, but why are we here?"

Rabi asked. "Because, Rabi, Our lord here, is a long time member of the club in question. According to my sources in London he is known to be as straight as they come. Also if the murders, as we believe are connected to someone in the club, someone with great power and influence may be needed to support us and give us a measure of protection, and you never know we may even get a tip-off or two." This thought intrigued Rabi.

Further, he was unsure what would happen next, but this could be very exciting. On the other hand, he thought it might prove to be a waste of time, "These types of people all stick together," he told Tom, not wanting to get his hopes up. "We will see," Tom countered, and brushing his shoes on the back of his trouser legs, he asked Rabi if his boots were clean; Rabi followed suit, not wanting to be caught out. They climbed the steps to the front door; Tom signalled to Rabi to pull the long chain to his right, which rang a bell both inside and outside. It was not long before the large, heavy door opened enough to see the house's butler standing before them. Tom thought to himself, *the gatekeeper to the palace and all the secrets contained within.*

"Good morning, sirs; how may I help you?" The butler asked, looking straight at them without a smile on his face. Tom did not want to smile either, preferring to keep a more dignified and important look.

"My name is inspector Richards of Scotland yard, and this is my constable and driver, Rabi. Could you please inform his lordship that we are here on important business and that we need to speak with him as a matter of urgency?"

"Is he expecting you, sir?" The butler replied.

Tom was not so easily deterred, "I am sure if you inform his lordship that I am here, he will insist on seeing me now." Tom rebutted, trying hard not to be too pushy whilst still firm.

"Wait here, and I will see if he is available to see you." The butler was about to close the door on Tom and Rabi when lord Sexton stepped forward.

"It is ok, thank you, I was not sure what time they may come, if at all today." The door opened further to reveal that lord Sexton was indeed standing there. He smiled and welcomed Tom and Rabi into the hall and, simultaneously, asked his butler.

"Please, could you bring a fresh pot of tea for the two gentlemen? I believe they have come a long way. We will take it in the conservatory, oh, and perhaps a few biscuits as well, please." The butler replied, "certainly, sir, as you wish." The butler left the three of them standing in the hallway.

"Follow me," lord sexton asked as he walked down the hallway towards the conservatory. He led them through one room and into another where two large doors stood; one was slightly ajar, the other closed firmly. As they entered the conservatory, lord Sexton introduced his guests to Jane.

"Inspector Richards, this is my daughter, lady Jane Vincent and of course, inspector Richards's driver, constable Rabi." Tom was a little taken aback. He had not expected to see Jane standing there. Nor to have been introduced so formally. Surely lord Sexton knew precisely who he was and that Jane and himself already were acquainted with each other. Tom thought as he stepped forward to shake her ladyship's hand formally.

The whole experience of this charade was purely for Rabi's benefit, the only person here who did not know of the connections.

"It is an honour to meet you, my lady." Lord Sexton Stepped up the pretence further. He suggested that the constable might be more comfortable with his tea in the garden whilst he awaited the inspector to conclude his business with them. Rabi was not so sure; he had no idea what was unfolding in front of him, each player in this pantomime took their turn without prompt or script seamlessly as if it had been choreographed and rehearsed previously.

Tom turned to Rabi with a slight wink of his eye and suggested, "this might be of some benefit as I should not be here too long." Rabi felt more comfortable leaving the room, knowing Tom would divulge the details in the car on the way home; that is what he hoped. The room fell silent as Rabi picked up his tea and a few biscuits for good company, leaving everyone to their conversation.

When the door closed behind Rabi, Jane could barely contain herself from showing a great deal of emotion. However, she knew Rabi could see her through the windows and decided to only voice her great excitement at seeing Tom again. "I am so glad you came, thank you, Tom, so very much," Jane had allowed her composure to drop enough to enable both Tom and her father to see how pleased she was.

Tom replied, "how could I not come and visit? Although I must admit, I did not expect to see you today; I am very glad we are both here." Before Tom could say any more. Jane's father interrupted them both, saying.

"Before we all get carried away with reunions, as touching as they are, please let us all remember why we are here. Tom, as we have already said, we are grateful that you have decided to come in person, especially as it is a very long way for you."

Tom just smiled as Jane's father continued to talk. "If you had telephoned ahead, we might have made some better plans for you, or perhaps if you had sent the letter back as requested letting us know your decision." Lord Sexton paused for a moment longer than he might have intended, perhaps out of respect for Tom. It may have been his failing health that, for a brief moment, had got the better of him. Tom mistook this pause as if lord Sexton was using it as a way to let Tom know that he had perhaps put a step wrong and was now being corrected. Due to this thought, Tom began to explain why he had not returned the letter or had not replied.

"Yes, the letter, lord Sexton," Tom said. "I have only just received it this very morning. The day it was delivered to my home address; I had already been seconded here to Edinburgh to work on a dreadful case of the two girls that had been murdered. You may have read about them in the newspapers."

Tom had decided to assume nothing here at this stage to try and gauge how much the others knew first. He continued his explanation by saying, "after speaking to Mary, my wife, a few days later. She said I had some personal letters, so I asked her to post them to me when she had a few minutes. Unfortunately, due to our daughters' health, this was put off longer than anticipated."

Tom paused, fearing he was saying too much; however, both Jane and her father said nothing allowing him to continue further. "By the time Mary had posted the letter to me, I was already on my way back to see my family. The letter was here in Edinburgh, and I was back home until today. Hence once I picked up the letter and read it, I knew my duty was to come straight here in the hope that you would forgive the unannounced intrusion." Tom stopped talking; he was not about to beg forgiveness for a situation that was not under his control. Besides, they were in greater need of him, not the other way around.

Jane's eyes never left off gazing at Tom the whole time; she had already forgiven him when she saw him again. Lord Sexton replied, "I understand, Tom, you could not have known the importance of the letter and family is important to you, I can see that, that is why I am sure you are possibly the only person that can help resolve this whole sorry situation, speaking of the letter do you have it with you?" Tom replied, "yes, I have it here with me!" He put his hand inside his jacket pocket and pulled out the letter. "Excellent, good man, I knew I could rely on you. Could you please pass it to me?"

Tom did as requested and handed it to lord Sexton, "thank you, Tom; I am sorry to do this, Jane. However, this is important." After saying that, Jane's father struck a match and burned the entire letter, placing the ashes into an ashtray by the window. Tom was a little taken aback by this; he had hoped to reread it later, as he had not had a chance to digest all that Jane had said. And he hoped that more might be told between the lines; Jane, on the other hand, understood completely.

"Why have you asked for my help, as the letter does not divulge that information, as far as I can see?" Tom had decided now to take control of the situation. Jane wanted to speak candidly to Tom and perhaps just might have done that. "I think in the interests of the sensitivity of your case, it would be best that we speak later today. Perhaps just the three of us without your driver; would you like to come here, let's say at four o'clock today, then we can speak more freely, and after we can all have dinner together. I am sure you and Jane will have a lot of catching up together."

Jane added, "that would be lovely, does that suit you, Tom?" Tom agreed that this might be the best option for everyone, and it would at least give him a chance to dig deeper into what they know. "Will there be a dress code for dinner?" Tom inquired, "or as I am?" Tom hoped it would not be formal; he did not like that sort of thing. "No, as you are will be perfectly acceptable, thank you for asking, we will send a car for you at 3 O'clock which will give you enough time to do whatever you need and bring you back to ours. Also, I am sure it may prove to be a long night, so we will have a guest room made up for you, then my driver can take you back in the morning ready for work." Tom did not want to disagree with the plans; after all, it is not every day you get to stay somewhere so grand.

Tom thanked lord Sexton and Jane for their hospitality and assured them he would do whatever he could in connection to whatever they were about to discuss that evening. He then signalled Rabi to go and get the car started as they were about to be leaving. Rabi re-entered the room. He thanked lord Sexton and his daughter for their hospitality. He followed the butler, who had also re-entered the room very soon after Jane's father had rung a discrete bell to the side of his chair. The butler took Rabi back to where the car had been parked earlier; neither said a word to each other as they walked along the hallway.

"Just one thing more," Jane's father asked Tom, "Is your investigation moving forward?" Tom did not know what to make of the question, so he replied positively, "So far, we have made some good advances and I have someone in custody in connection to the murders, however, we charging him with different offences currently." "Perhaps this evening we can talk more on that subject?"

Tom nodded his head in agreement, taking that the statement from lord Sexton about his case and Jane's letter were very much connected.

Tom got into the car with Rabi, "I think we need to go back to the station so we can decide upon our next course of action, hopefully, George will be back and we can have another look at what we have learned, and see what evidence we have collected."

"Well Rabi, that was an interesting situation, would you not agree?"

"It was sir." Rabi was curious about what was said when he was politely ordered from the room, he did not want to be presumptuous, but inside he was bursting to find out.

"Would you like to know what just happened Rabi?"

"yes, I am very confused, did we learn much, was it all worthwhile? I only seemed to get some odd looks, a cup of tea and some biscuits, not to mention freezing my..." Rabi stopped talking without finishing the sentence; he thought he might have gone too far with what he was about to say.

Tom was not worried or put off by Rabi's tone of voice or choice of words. "It's ok, Rabi to be frustrated by it all, I would be also, however, there are some things we both have learned. first, though, why do you think they may have directed you outside of the room?" Rabi kept silent as he thought for a few moments and then replied, "I do not know why except that they think they're better than me because I am only a constable and your driver!" Tom could tell Rabi was very irritated by all of this, so Tom helped him with his reasoning by saying, "You are right, they believe you are not important to the case and that is a good thing."

"I don't understand why?" Rabi replied, looking very confused.

"It is a good thing because they do not know how much you know about the case, they are not aware of the important role you have played, that point will give us an advantage." Tom went on to explain. However, Rabi was still very confused about why this would be an advantage. So Tom continued by saying.

"They do not know what investigations you have made on my behalf. They may be inclined to think that whatever they tell me is the real truth, not knowing we may already know because of your hard work." Rabi had now begun to understand the point and looked less uncomfortable and unhappy about being shut out.

"So, what else have we learned then, sir?" Rabi asked in a more positive mood.

"Well, we have also learned that as they blocked you from the conversation, they have information that is sensitive and will need handling carefully. Information that they do not want getting out easily. This also means I will have to revisit them very soon to find out what that might be."

Rabi smiled, "you see, Rabi, sometimes you have to look past what is being said and look at what is not; this often gives us more than people realise." It was not long before they were back at the station; Rabi had learned enough not to discuss the case as they walked through the station until they had reached their murder room, as Tom was now calling it.

"Well done, by the way," Tom said as they returned to their room.

"What for, sir?" "Taking the initiative to lock this room before you left, I presume it was you, not George."

Tom decided that after all that Rabi had just gone through, the least he could do was give a little praise, especially when it was well deserved. This improved Rabi's mood further, "that's better, Rabi, chin up and let's keep going; perhaps George will be back soon with more information as well."

Time seemed to pass quicker now that Rabi was in a better mood, and Tom had at least seen Jane, albeit unexpectedly. He was unsure how this evening would pan out or what information lord Sexton would divulge to him. Even Tom had to admit this thought would give him that slight butterfly feeling many of us get when we mix a little nervousness and excitement together.

It was not long before George returned to give a full report of his morning's work. Rabi welcomed him back enthusiastically, "Hi George, how did it go? have you got any juicy or interesting information for us?"

Tom smiled at Rabi's enthusiasm, adding, "How did it go?"

"It was a little frustrating, most people did not want to talk to me too much, but then they were busy working, but I did find out a few things that are interesting, I can read you back my notes if you like?"

From previous experience, Tom knew it may prove to be a challenge so he commended him for his persistence and said, "we can all have a show and tell in just a few moments we need to recap on our board first and see what blanks we can fill in."

Chapter Twenty-Three

The Murder Room

"All right then, let's go through in order, all that we know, so far. We need to keep this in a logical order. First we know that the girl's deaths did not occur where we found their bodies because there were no signs of misadventure or struggle, and the girls were too neatly arranged. What don't we know about the girls?"

There was a long silence; neither Rabi nor George knew the answer to Tom's question. Tom closed the silence gap by saying. "We do not have the post-mortem results for the girls. We need to know the exact cause of death and the time when they died. So far, all we have done is assume that because each of the girls had a large amount of bruising around their throats, it was murder by strangulation. This has to be verified and confirmed."

This thought had not crossed either of the constable's minds; why would they, of course, they are not detectives yet.

"I think I need to contact the coroner's office to chase up on those reports; that has to be a matter of urgency." Tom was annoyed that he had allowed what was happening around him and the case to distract him. He knew if he could see a preliminary report, he would be able to work out approximate timelines and possible causes rather than assume. "Remember this, lads, never assume; it will always make an Ass of U and Me." Both Rabi and George were unsure whether to smile or not, so instead opted for that knowing look and nodded, hoping to show solidarity in thinking.

Rabi then chimed in by adding, "Sir we do know of course the girl's backgrounds and why James recruited them; for the sole purpose of these so-called parties for the toffs." George then added, "We also know that there was a party not too long ago at the club. I found out it was private, invites only and that it was organised by lord Vincent. Sir, I found out something that is very disturbing."

George was not sure what to say. He did not know all the details or who it was. However, he continued, "well, sir, it would appear that one of our own, a police officer was present at the party; I do not know his name yet. However, it is rumoured to be a detective."

The room was stunned into silence. After what had seemed a few minutes. Tom broke the silence asking, "that's not good news, it brings suspicion back to the station, we must be extra careful whom we speak too and what about, this could derail our entire case, we need to speak to James again and see if he was privileged to that sort of information."

Suddenly and very unexpectedly, there was a knock on the door; George was sitting the closest, so he got up and opened it just enough to see who it was.

"Hi, Pete, what's up?" George asked.

"The chief put in a request for a telephone to be installed in here, apparently he was tired of receiving calls for the English inspector or being disturbed when he needed to make a private call himself."

Pete had brought with him a workman to install the telephone line.

"Is it ok to install it now or are you busy, it won't take five minutes?"

Tom, who could hear every word being and said, "let them in, George; this English detective inspector could do with his own phone." Tom was being a little sarcastic, which made George and Rabi smile. However, Pete now felt a little foolish for speaking out. Pete mistakenly thought George was on his own. They stopped talking about the case and quickly covered all evidence they had received. The workman said nothing at all; he diligently installed the phone, pulling a cable out from the ceiling and down to Tom's desk; after a quick check to make sure the phone was working, both Pete and the man left the room and apologised for disturbing them briefly.

"That is handy; we can make excellent use of that now," Rabi said, perhaps thinking of making one or two private calls at some point. Tom knew what Rabi meant; he would not pull him up on it, preferring to say, "no phoning your mothers in Australia," and make light of it all. Tom then changed the subject to their inquiry, saying, "Do you know when this party took place?" "Yes, sir, it was only two days before the girl's bodies were discovered." Tom became very interested in this fact, "can we prove the two girls were there that night?"

"Yes sir I found two eyewitnesses confirming this fact, and I am sure that James will confirm he sent them to the party."

Tom's mind began to work quickly, racing with everything he needed to do and confirm. "Rabi, could you please use our newly installed telephone and get me through to the coroner's office? I need to speak with him urgently, and George, could you please arrange for James to be brought to an interview room? I want to talk with him as soon as possible after my call. Thank you, lads; great work so far. Let's keep this going and remember not a word to anyone."

Before Rabi could pick up the phone to make his call, it rang rather loudly, surprising them all; Rabi picked up the receiver and asked who was there. "Hello, can I speak to inspector Richards please?"

"Can I ask who is calling please?"

"His London office!" the voice said rather rudely.

Tom picked up the phone cautiously, saying, "can I help you, inspector Richards speaking." It was not long before Tom recognised the voice on the phone to be not someone from his London office but rather the reporter from the London tribune.

"I have the information you requested, sir, and I am not sure you will like it, but it may help you solve your murder case. All the members of the club are not connected necessarily, but they all have things very much in common. To start, you have to be rich and well connected business-wise, but that is very common for these types of clubs; the second is you cannot apply to be a member; you may only be invited and then approved by the committee to get a full lifetime membership. You only get removed from the club if you go bankrupt or are found guilty of criminal offences." Bernie paused to allow

Tom to take all this in before continuing his report. "Here is where it gets fascinating from my point of view; lord Vincent is the chairman, and he by all rights should be disbarred from being there as his business is under investigation for fraud, it would appear that he has very high debts and no means to pay them. Lord Vincent is only still a member because his wife has her own money and position, which is controlled by her father, lord Sexton. He of course is another long-time member and a wealthy and powerful man with many connections here, including government; it is rumoured he is on the team looking into abolishing capital punishment. My favourite story as well you know sir." "Thank you, Bernie, this is very helpful to my case."

"That is not all, though; here is the bit you may not like very much. First, there are two members, one full and the other temporary, currently serving members of the police force there in Edinburgh. The first of these, the full permanent member, is a high-ranking officer who has family money so is considered rich enough and probably does not need to work. He will likely be your boss there, so you might want to be extra careful. The second is more disturbing as he is only a detective and has minimal financial means. All this can only mean one thing in my book, he is being sponsored, but the big question is why? Tom's heart sank. He thought he almost knew before he asked the question, "do you have the name of that detective Bernie?"

"I do; it is a man you are very well acquainted with," before Bernie could continue, Tom said, "is it Bob! he works here and is working on a big fraud case at the moment?"

Bernie replied, "I am afraid so, sorry to be the bearer of bad news, but you need to know and watch your back, especially if he asks you questions; I am sure I don't need to tell you that."

The news devastated Tom; he had to entertain the idea that his old friend was now a corrupt police officer. He was possibly subverting a fraud case to benefit one of his suspects. He may now have to consider that Bob may be involved in the murders. All this for what reason? Only to gain a measure of power and influence and perhaps make some money simultaneously. Tom felt sick to his stomach at this thought and was unsure how much information to divulge to

Rabbi and George. They needed protection for their careers; at least he could go home when this was all over, and he was looking to have this as his last case so he could retire and spend more time with his family.

Tom's next thought was, just how much of this information does Jane or her father know, are either of them protecting lord Vincent and that is the real reason for him being asked to help them. Tom pondered these thoughts as he thanked Bernie for all his hard work, "Is our deal still in place for the exclusive on this inspector?" Bernie asked. Tom did not want to be short with Bernie but just replied, "yes," before hanging up the phone.

"Are you all right, Sir?" Rabi asked, "you seem very disturbed by that call. Is it your family? If it is, we can hold the fort if you need to get back to them." Rabi felt very concerned for Tom at this point as Tom did not say a word; he was in deep thought as to his next move. "They are all right; it was not about my family, thanks. We will need to be very careful; I believe I know who the police officer is, who attended that party, and he could be very dangerous."

At that moment, George arrived back in the office, "that's all set up for you, sir; he is in interview room one waiting for you." he paused, sensing something had just happened, "what's up? What did I miss?" George became very curious.

Rabi replied, "the inspector has just received a phone call from London with some disturbing information. It would appear our boss may know the other police officer who attended that party as a guest; I think he works here."

George looked shocked and stood there in silence; Rabi stopped talking, suddenly panicking and thinking he may have just told the one person that he should not. Tom looked at them both, realising the situation and said, "I know that it was not either of you; it is ok. Don't start suspecting each other; the other officer is someone I once worked with a long time ago."

Rabi felt a little relief; he did not want to start suspecting his new friend and colleague. George felt the same by the look on his face; then the thought came to him, "if it is not them, then who?" Rabi spoke up and said, "sir, the first night you were here, I dropped you off at a friend's house for dinner. Is it him?" Rabi was trying to be diplomatic but felt he needed to know; however, he thought George should hear it from Tom's mouth and did not want to usurp him in any way. Tom nodded his head whilst still in deep thought and replied. "Yes, Rabi, you are right; I believe the other officer is..." he paused, almost not wanting to say his name out loud, but then continued by simply saying, "Bob!"

"Does this mean he is our number one suspect, and how will you proceed with that investigation? "George asked; he understood the implications all too well, as did Rabi, "No one likes a dirty officer!" he exclaimed. Tom added, "that is why we will not say anything about this outside of this room; only we can know this until the right time. We still need that report, Rabi, if you could chase that up for me, perhaps collect it in person, for my eyes only. Remember, this is for your protection as well."

Tom was deep in thought about Bob, how he had tried to re-kindle a friendship from the past. Now Tom felt sick; his friend and colleague wanted to betray him. Worse still, perhaps frame him. Tom knew that he would have to put that to one side and dig deep, "come on Tom, put your big boy pants on!" he thought to himself, "there is work to be done."

George said, "Sir, I do not mean to point out the obvious; however, James is still in interview room one."

"Thank you, right let's get this over with; I want, no! I need this case over with; it is starting to irritate me now. I can not abide injustice or deceit, Rabi; you know what you have to do, George. You come with me."

Tom had changed his attitude and become more brusque. Not enough to be completely rude to all around him, but enough to show he now meant business. Tom would not suffer fools or be fobbed off with weak, feeble or inaccurate statements designed to protect themselves. It was almost as if someone had turned on a switch inside him.

Tom and George walked into the interview room where James was sitting, "sorry to have kept you waiting. Has anyone got you a cup of tea, or would you prefer coffee?" Tom had changed tac the moment he entered the room, well that is how had appeared to George. "So, James." George was unsure about this sudden change, so he decided to listen and take notes. Tom paused for effect, "do you remember that big file I brought in previously?" Tom did not wait for James to reply; he just continued speaking. "Well, here is the long and short of it; that file is now so large, I can not carry it, and my constable here says that he does not want to hurt his back picking it up; that is how much evidence we now have against you. In the interests of being fair, though, I would like to share some snippets, as it were, with you, and if you want, feel free to comment on them, and we can have a friendly chat; how does that sound?

Tom was well acquainted with this cat and mouse game and had played it many times. On the other hand, he could see that James was not comfortable; he was fidgeting in his chair. As Tom began speaking, he suddenly sat forward and looked straight at Tom and replied, "Yes, If I do cooperate can you give me protection inside?" He answered by saying. "Well, if it were my decision alone then I would do everything in my power. I must be honest with you, though, James, it depends on the answers you give me and how much you cooperate. You see, I have a boss too, we call him the chief, have you met him? He is a very tall man, very strong-minded and does not like people messing him around." Tom liked to pause after making statements like this; it often gave the suspect time to think about this and let it settle in.

Jame's attitude had changed completely; it was evident to everyone in the room; that you could see that he was scared. The question is, was he scared by what Tom had just said and decided to cooperate, or was something else disturbing him? Tom needed to push a little harder to check this out. Tom continued, "the thing with the chief is, he is well connected. Does that worry you, James? James replied quickly, "I know about your chief, and no, he is not the person that worries me the most; at least if I help you, he has the power to help me."

Tom knew by this statement that the only other person who would worry James could be Bob! Tom decided to tell James he knew about the other detective who could create problems by saying. "That is an interesting statement, James; however, I know someone else is involved here. Has this person threatened you since you have been in our custody?" James became a little paler at this question and very uncomfortable. "What on earth makes you think that someone has threatened me? I am not easily intimidated as well, you know, and besides all of that, I have been in here all this time."

James had decided to try and bluff his way through this interview. He did not want to appear weak, particularly if he was going to prison; he needed his reputation to be tough. "That is all commendable, James, and of course, you are right; you are a tough man, but there is always someone bigger and stronger; it is a simple fact of life, as I'm sure you know."

James smiled and looked Tom straight in the eye, saying, "and I am sure you know, the bigger they are, the harder they can fall, and those that tell stories about dirty coppers get.., well, you know the rest." Tom realised James would not say more at this stage, but he was good at reading between the lines; he knew James had been referring to Bob, although neither had wanted to say that name out loud. Both knew, of course, that no matter what was said out loud, the words not spoken were the loudest of all.

"When was the first time you were approached to provide girls and other services such as the drugs? Or did you approach the club first?" Tom continued in his interview by changing the focus of the discussion and directing the questions more toward the club.

James seemed happier to talk about this subject matter more and replied, "I was approached first, my uncle served under lord Vincent, his reputation, my uncle's that is was that he could obtain almost anything from anywhere for the right price, so after the war he continued in this same business only for a little profit for himself. My uncle took me under his wing, so to speak and showed me all his ways and tricks. So when lord Vincent needed some help, naturally he came to me since my uncle is not around anymore. Then one thing led to another and he asked me about supplying girls for his "special parties," as he called them, I was never allowed to attend but the girls were to be young, keen to party and enjoy themselves and not ask questions so naturally, if they are not so clever they will not think for themselves and skim from the drugs I would later give them to supply to the gentleman being entertained by them.

I personally think that lord Vincent was using his parties to make connections and money. I think he is struggling financially."

Tom already knew some of this information, but it was helpful to hear it, "Will you swear to this in a written statement?" He asked directly.

"Yes, if it helps get me a deal and protection, would that be enough?"

"Well it is certainly a good start, however, I will need a lot more information to go to my chief to ask for a deal."

"Like what?"

"Well, how about the names of the people that were at the last party, and whilst we are talking, do you know who killed the two girls, that would be very helpful?"

Tom was trying to put James in a more relaxed state of mind to get him talking more. "I'm afraid I am not privileged to the guest list for these parties, but I can tell you some of the names for the last one. I also know your chief has never been to these parties, he would never be invited. Lord Vincent only wants people with business connections and money that will help him. Besides he does not like your chief, but then having said that your chief doesn't like lord Vincent, there is definitely no love lost there between them."

James seemed happier and more relaxed talking. "Have you ever seen lord Vincent taking money from these party invites, James?" James could not say for sure if this ever happened. However, he did confirm that lord Vincent arranged everything and insisted that only the girls take the drugs into the parties. He never wanted to handle them, and "he always paid me in cash the next day. I am happy to put that in writing, too, if that helps."

Tom was pleased with this statement, "Yes, this will help a lot, how about lord Sexton has he ever attended these parties?" Tom wanted to make sure before his meeting tonight with him, just in case.

"No, they're not fans of each other either, I think, from what I understand they fell out over his daughter's inheritance, he will not let her have it until lord Vincent can prove himself financially, it's funny don't you think, when you need money, no one will give you any, but when you don't, everyone wants to give it to you."

Tom agreed; he understood what James meant. Although, Tom had never been the kind of person to borrow money or spend more than he had.

"You have been very helpful; I am sure we can arrange something for you, just one more thing before I go, what do you know about the two girls deaths?" Tom asked.

"I..." James paused; Tom could see James looked very stressed and uncomfortable but said nothing waiting for James to speak.

"I would not be surprised if the girl's deaths were not deliberate and more accidental. I would also consider the possibility that their deaths did not happen where you found them or at the club, but they were moved by someone who knows you!"

Tom was startled a little by this comment, James knew what happened, and this was a big hint towards what had happened. Armed with this information, he may have even solved the case. Just then, there was a knock on the door. "Come in," Tom called.

Rabi came walking in clutching a manilla folder, "sir," he whispered in a low tone, "I have the report you wanted right here."

"Have you looked at it yet, Rabi?" Tom was keen to find out what it said, "no sir, your eyes only, remember." Although Rabi had wanted to peek inside, he thought it was not the right thing to do, preferring to follow Tom's instructions earlier.

"Good man," Tom replied, "Thank you."

Rabi took his leave of the room but not before asking if there was anything else he could do. "Not for now, Rabi; you can call it a day; we will reconvene in the morning; it is time I spoke to the chief." Turning to look James directly in the eye, Tom said, "This is a full report of the autopsy for both the girls; I am sure it will make fascinating reading."

James never said a word until George decided to speak. "If there is anything else you want to add, now would be a good time, particularly if you want to change anything you have said." Tom was secretly impressed by George; he had kept quiet until now, preferring to observe the situation. Tom underlined what George had just said by saying. "I will speak with you tomorrow, giving you the night to consider all we have spoken about. In the morning, I will speak to the chief to see what we can do for you. Thank you for your cooperation, James." James just looked at them both and then asked as Tom and George left the room, "is there a visitors log when coming to see a prisoner?" Tom turned to him and asked, "why, do you ask that?" James never replied, preferring to look directly at Tom once more. Tom knew it was a loaded question and chose not to push further; he nodded and walked away. "What was that all about?" George asked, becoming very curious. Tom did not want to say it directly. Instead, he asked George to check all visitor logs since James came into custody then he could go home.

Tom turned to the custody sergeant and asked how long he was on duty. "I have only just come on shift, sir." Tom thought for a moment, "ok, do not let anyone else go into his cell, only you until I come back in the morning, is that clear? No one!" Tom was perhaps a little too forceful in his speech towards the custody sergeant. However, he needed to impress on him the importance without saying why. Tom looked at his watch and realised it was almost time to go, the car would be here for him soon, and he wanted to let the chief know they needed to speak.

Tom hurried to the chief's office, knocked on the door and barely waited for the chief to ask him in; "Tom, I did not expect to see you; what's up? "Sir, something has come up in my investigation that you need to know, and it is not good news at all!" Tom knew that things would become complicated when he told the chief about the corrupt officer and said his name out loud.

"Sir, first of all, I have a meeting with Lord Sexton this evening. I knew his daughter in London and I believe they have information that will help us. However, it is very sensitive, and I am sure he is an honest and trustworthy man. I'm reliably informed he still carries out work for her majesty's government now. However, during the war he worked on some very discreet and difficult missions for the good of us all." "So why are you telling me this now?" The chief asked, looking very annoyed that he was finding out this. "Sir, I want to give you a full brief in the morning if that is all right with you. In the meantime, I have instructed the custody sergeant that no one goes into see my prisoner except me if that is all right." The chief agreed, asking, "Does it look bad on this station? Do I need to escalate things?" "Not yet, sir; we need kid gloves right now, especially as it involves the club you belong to, yourself, lord Sexton and Lord Vincent. One thing I know and think is worth saying at this point; I am convinced, sir, that you are not involved and would be very happy to see this whole mess come to fruition."

"Thank you, Tom, for the vote of confidence," He replied in an almost sarcastic way but continued to say, "So, I can expect a full report in the morning then?"

"Yes Sir, I should be in a much better position to speak more freely in the morning."

"All right Tom, get to you're meeting and we can speak tomorrow."

Tom agreed and felt he had the confidence of the chief. Just as Tom was about to leave, a constable appeared to tell them that there was a car waiting out the front for Tom.

Chapter Twenty-Four

The house of Sexton

Tom left the chief's office and followed the constable to where the car was waiting for him. Standing before him was a man dressed exactly as one might expect a chauffeur to look. This includes the grey suit, white shirt and a black tie with a flat cap standing at the passenger side of a Rolls Royce with the door open. Tom looked a little embarrassed; he was not used to such a situation, especially as it was at his place of work; he was sure tongues would wag after this.

He got into the car and asked the driver to take him to the B & B, where he could pick up a few things for his overnight stay at the house of lord Sexton. They soon pulled up outside; it was as if the driver had already known where he had been living and was familiar with the route. "Here we are, sir," the driver said. "If you wait just a moment, I can get the door for you." If Tom had felt a little embarrassed before, now he felt somewhat uncomfortable. He was barely out of the car when Han, the landlady, opened the front door to greet Tom. "Good afternoon Han; how are you?" Tom said as he walked toward her; Han could hardly keep her eyes away from the car when she replied, "I am doing very well, thank you, clearly though not as well as you, sir." Han was hoping to find out why Tom had arrived in the chauffeur-driven Rolls Royce. "Oh, I know, it certainly is unconventional for someone like me to be driven around in this manner, but I must say it is very comfortable. Don't worry though, I have not gone up in the world, the car and driver are both courtesy of my host for tonight, which is why I am here; I have to collect a couple of things from my room, it is doubtful I will be back tonight as I have an early start in the morning. It will probably be very late tonight when I finish."

Tom did not want to say too much. However, he felt Han deserved some explanation and tried to assure her that the room would still be paid for in the usual manner.

"Well, all I will say is Don't work too hard, your lordship. Oh, and please remember us, mere mortals!" Han said, giggling and looking very excited about the chauffeur-driven car. Tom did not hang around long when he collected his overnight bag. He preferred to throw a few things into a small suitcase while hurrying back to the car waiting for him.

Apprehension was now beginning to overtake Tom as he sat in the back of the car again. The questions kept coming to his mind, one after the other, without cessation. His mind began to consider all the possibilities that might happen this evening; how would lord Sexton react towards him? What would both he and Jane say to each other? What was essential to the house of Sexton that Jane was compelled to write after all these years? And what did this have to do with Tom's case? All these questions and thoughts distracted him from his journey enough not to realise he had already arrived at his destination. The car pulled up along the front of the house where Jane was already waiting for him. The driver opened the door to the car and waited patiently for Tom to exit the vehicle. "Thank you, driver, for your help," Tom did not know what to say to him; however, he did feel obliged to at least recognise his work and skill and thought that the least he could say was, "thank you."

Tom moved towards the open door where Jane had been patiently waiting in excitement and anticipation "welcome Tom," she said as he approached her. "Daddy is waiting in his study for us; I have already asked the maid to organise some tea and cake as a light refreshment; dinner will be served at 7 pm." Tom did not know what to say except, "That will be lovely, thank you, Jane."

"So, Tom, I can not believe you are here; thank you for coming. You must tell me all about your life in London, how you met Mary, your wife, and of course your little girl, her name is Emily isn't it? How is she doing? is there anything I can do to help her? I understand she is rather poorly at the moment and in hospital." Tom felt quite overwhelmed by the enthusiastic welcome he had received from Jane. "Look at me bombarding you with all these questions; I am sorry, Tom, it is just so good to see you." Jane took him by his arm as though they had never been apart and the last ten years had not happened, "Daddy's study is through here." She continued as she knocked on the door and waited for confirmation to enter.

After being beckoned in, Jane began to speak, "Daddy, look, Tom has arrived ready, and I am sure very willing to help." Lord Sexton interrupted her, saying.

"Thank you, Tom, for coming; I appreciate all this must be somewhat problematic and perhaps overwhelming, but it is excellent to see you again. Jane, have you asked the kitchen for some refreshments?" Yes, I have already done so; I have also asked for some of that lovely lemon cake we have to be brought in as well; I remember how Tom loves a piece of cake." It was at that moment The refreshments arrived. Jane politely dismissed the maid in favour of pouring and serving the tea herself. She wanted to ensure that Tom was as comfortable as possible; she knew there was a lot at stake for everyone.

As Jane served the tea and cake, she asked her father, "should I stay, or would you prefer to speak to Tom, man to man, daddy?" Jane hoped she would be allowed to stay; she wanted to spend as much time as possible with Tom catching up. "I think, for now, my dear, we can all stay together and talk, then after dinner, perhaps Tom and I can speak alone for a while privately; how does that sound to everyone?" Tom could not say. Otherwise, this was not his home, and he was the guest; Jane, on the other hand, was delighted by this plan.

"I want you to know, Tom, that whatever is spoken about here between us will stay that way strictly. Not a word will be spoken to others. I do hope that we can be afforded the same courtesy and discretion?"

Lord Sexton paused. The silence became a little uncomfortable for a moment; not even Jane spoke, and then Tom replied, "of course, I can assure you of my complete discretion. I must also assure you, during the course of this discussion or indeed the whole evening, if you or Jane tell me anything that is pertinent to my case. Equally, if you have foreknowledge of a crime or perhaps knowledge after the fact, I am dutybound by my oath to the crown to act on this and perhaps use this information as evidence. To gain justice on behalf of the deceased girls and their families." Tom had decided to make things clear from the outset that although he and Jane were old friends, he would not let this get in the way of his duty. "Excellent! that is exactly what I wanted to hear; thank you, Tom, for your courage and forthrightness. This is what we need to resolve this situation.

Do you believe the two girls' deaths are murder or misadventure?" "That is a good question; as of yet, I have not seen the autopsy report and cannot say with certainty either way. What do you know about this situation?" Tom decided to turn the question around. He knew he had the report and was planning to read it before work in the morning, so technically, Tom had not lied. He did not want to let on about his suspicions in case things backfired on him.

"Well, that is what we want to talk to you about. According to the newspapers, Jane told me girls were found in a manner that resembled your murders from 1945. I looked into that, and I am convinced without a shadow of a doubt that they are not connected! I know about some of the details from the original case, even though they were never made public. I also believe that someone here has decided to make it appear that they are connected, which puts you in a very difficult position." Tom listened intently to what lord Sexton was saying. He was not shocked at the information and knew he was very well connected to all the right people. Lord Sexton continued, "There are connections here in Scotland you may not be aware of Tom. Connections that have deliberately set out to harm you; however, the result could cost you your reputation and career if you are not careful."

"What connections are you referring to?" Lord Sexton did not want to say initially as he was trying to gauge how much Tom knew so far.

"Before I get to that, What do you know about the club and its members, Tom?" Tom hesitated for a moment before saying, "I know you are a member, and I also know Jane's husband, lord

Vincent, is also a member. There are a few other surprise members." Tom stopped to allow for any comments from Jane or her father.

Tom continued, "my enquiries have revealed that you are above suspicion due to your past and current work within Her majesty's government. Most of which I know you can not talk about, and quite frankly, I am not sure I would want to know anyway. I am also aware that my boss here, the chief as he is referred to, is also a member, and I know that neither you nor he is particularly fond of lord Vincent, I am sorry to say that Jane." Jane looked at Tom and replied, "It is true things have been very strained recently, which is another reason we require your help!" Jane's father stepped in, adding. "Your very well-informed Tom. Are you aware why?"

Tom tried to be more diplomatic by replying, "from what I understand, his recent actions at the club and financial dealings are causing some irritation and friction."

Tom knew he needed to be careful here. He did not want to upset Jane or alienate her father; he needed both of them onside to tease more information. "That is putting it mildly; Jane and I want to level with you. We believe lord Vincent is using the club for illicit gains financially," Tom could see Jane becoming more upset at what was about to be said. "We believe the illicit gains made at the club are through these parties, parties in which girls are given out to the guests who sell drugs to other guests. Jane will imminently be filing for divorce, citing these accusations. We need the proof for her sake. However, we must also ensure discretion for her and our family name. We intend to present lord Vincent with our evidence so that he will not contest this and grant her a quick clean divorce."

Jane was now trying especially hard to hold back her tears, she did not want to break down in front of Tom completely, but this was proving very hard to achieve. "Jane, I am so sorry that you have found yourself in this situation through no fault of your own. This is very difficult for you, so please be assured that I will do all I can to help you." Tom felt very upset seeing the pain Jane was in. "Lord Sexton, do you have any other information to help the case? You see, I believe that lord Vincent is implicated in the girl's deaths, although I also believe that the girl's bodies were moved by someone else; I have my suspicions on who this person is; however, I still need proof, of course." Lord Sexton looked Tom square in the eyes and replied, "Tom, you have made a lot of progress in a short time; we need to discuss how you plan to move forward with this. I have a few ideas in this regard. Perhaps after dinner, we can discuss this better. For now, though, we should take a break if, for nothing else but Jane's sake, the time is now almost 6 pm, dinner is at 7 pm, so let us take a short break to freshen up a little, have a nice dinner then maybe for a while you and Jane could catch up and remember some of the better times you both enjoyed together."

Jane smiled a little at this thought; she needed to take a break to compose herself.

"Tom, I will have Andrews show you to your room, he has already taken your luggage from the car." Jane pressed a small button on the desk where her father sat to signal to the staff that assistance was required.

As Tom left the room, he turned once again to Jane and said," Jane, I am so sorry that you have to bear all this: let's all hope we can resolve this quickly and with the least pain for everyone." He followed Andrews through the hallway leading to the main staircase and his room.

Tom's room was not the kind of room he was used to. It had a large four-poster bed in the centre of one wall opposite the window that was draped with heavy curtains, and under the window stood a large writing desk with an assortment of paper, a pen and the telephone. He wondered if it was improper to use the phone to call Mary, his wife; he sat at the desk and pondered this for a few moments before deciding that it could not do any harm. He picked up the receiver and began dialling; it was not long before Mary answered, "Hello darling, it's me, Tom," he said softly. "How are you? How is Emily? Have you heard anything yet?" Tom could almost not bear being apart from his family any longer. However, Mary replied, "I am all right considering the circumstances. I have heard from the hospital this afternoon that Emily still is not out of the woods and is very poorly. However, she is sleeping well at night, and during the day, she is playing with some new friends she has made when she is up to it. It would seem our new friend, the reporter, has been of more help. He has a short news item to write for his paper on the hospital.

There is to be a dedication and service for a new building that has been built. He also says that if it is all right with you, I can come along, which might also mean I can get in to see Emily tomorrow; what do you think?"

Tom was happy to hear that Emily was settling in well. However, he was not so happy that his wife would be attending this event with a newspaper reporter, especially how it might look to others who may see this take place whilst he is away. Tom could not help himself feel this way, even though he was at Jane's father's house and would soon be having dinner and spending the night. With this all in mind and the fact he had not informed Mary, he reluctantly agreed; after all, this was not about his feelings. It was an opportunity for Mary to see their daughter and perhaps settle their minds.

"That sounds like a wonderful idea, if possible please hug her and kiss her from me. Mary, it might be best, especially for the sake of gossip, that you meet him away from the house though."

Tom felt duplicitous at his remarks and decided to tell Mary where he was, at least that he was staying at lord Sexton's family house.

"You should see my room; it even has a phone, which I am using to call you now. I had a chauffeur collect me from the station and bring me here, a butler who showed me to my room; I could get used to all this." He chuckled, trying to relieve his guilt, knowing he would be having dinner with Jane shortly.

"That sounds wonderful darling, don't get too comfortable, remember we only have a two-bedroom end terraced house in London, there would be no room for a maid or butler."

Mary had also begun to laugh at this thought and added, "don't forget we will soon be having that wonderful caravan holiday in Holt, Norfolk. I am not sure the maid or butler would appreciate us all cramped together; we would have to get another caravan just for them, and what if they were not married? That would never do as we need a third to keep things above board."

Tom laughed even more and added, "well I would suppose that the best thing is to keep things simple, let's not hire any of those people and do things for ourselves, we have got along just fine without them all this time, what do you think, darling?"

"Well," Mary replied, "you know best, you are the one enjoying such privileges at the moment, after all, I am just a simple woman, who likes simple things, just like you."

Mary paused, knowing that what she had just said could be taken two different ways; Tom could see the joke and replied, "Thank you, darling, you are the best."

"I know, that is why you were attracted to me, and not just for my cooking skills."

Both of them began to feel more at ease about the situation they found themselves in, "Ok darling, I should be on my way, I am here to work and I have an autopsy report to read before dinner is served, I love you."

At that moment, Tom realised he was saying this more than he had ever said before. Maybe it was because he had not spent so much time away from home since he married, or perhaps it was the guilt of not telling Mary all the information. Whichever it was, he knew just how much he loved her and wanted to be home as soon as possible.

"I love you more than all the butlers and maids in the world," Mary replied as Tom was about to hang up. He was unsure how to respond and just said in a soft voice, "me too." this was a new one for him; he had never heard Mary say anything like this before, and he liked it.

Tom hung up the phone and just sat there for a few minutes before looking around the room for his luggage. Tom could not see his bag until he checked the wardrobe, his suit, shirt and tie and been freshly pressed and hung neatly, with his bag directly underneath. Tom felt very uncomfortable at this; this was not something Tom would have had someone do for him. However, he consoled himself that this was lord Sexton's house, and he had different ways and chose not to make a big deal of it; after all, he was only here for one night; what harm could it do.

Tom reached down to his bag with a sudden panic; what if the staff had found the reports and taken them to lord Sexton. Tom looked inside, expecting to see them gone; phew, he thought as he pulled out both reports, they were still there and had not been tampered with as far as he could see. He took them to the desk where he had been sitting earlier and began to read them.

Tom lost track of time as he read and combed over them, absorbing every detail. There was a knock on his door. Tom looked up, hoping it was not Jane coming into his room; this would not be appropriate; his heart began to beat faster at this thought, "Come in," he called, not knowing what to do for the best. The door opened, and standing before him was the butler, "Sir, Lady Vincent asked me to remind you that you have fifteen minutes before dinner is served and also asked if you were ready would you like to meet her downstairs before going in, to dinner." "Thank you, tell me, should I change into the suit you had pressed for me before dinner?" Tom felt relief at this; he would not have known how to handle the situation otherwise.

Tom took the opportunity to ask. "That might be more applicable, sir. Shall I tell her you will be joining her very shortly?" "Yes, thank you, and thank you for pressing and hanging my clothes; I am not used to this service, thank you." Tom found himself saying thank you far more than perhaps Jane or her father might. "Excellent, sir; I will inform her directly." The butler could see that Tom was not accustomed to this style of living, and although he secretly liked him for this, he was not going to stop being so formal with him. Tom changed very quickly to meet Jane before dinner. He tried very hard as he left his room and walked down the imposing staircase to look composed. As if he belonged there, this was all to no avail. It was evident to everyone this was not the case, especially to Jane. While waiting for Tom at the bottom of the staircase, she was trying to look casual.

Jane took Tom by his arm, linking hers through his, "come on," she said, "we have a few minutes before dinner. Let's go into the conservatory and chat before daddy arrives and dinner is served." Tom was unsure what to make of Jane's forwardness but went along with her as they walked into the conservatory where he had first seen Jane earlier that day. "Do you ever think back to those halcyon days? when although the war was on, life had seemed more simple." Jane asked as they entered the conservatory. "Sometimes," he replied, "but then, we can't live in the past. Sometimes the decisions we make may not always be right at first, but then over time, things have a way of working themselves out for the best." As

Tom said this, he was thinking about the night he and Jane were waiting at the station. Now Tom was married to Mary and how he was so happy, despite the situation they were all in.

On the other hand, Jane thought Tom was referring to the decision she had made to marry lord Vincent. Now that things were not working out, perhaps all would be good again in the future. Either way, although their friendship had paused seemingly forever, it was clear that they could both renew this tonight over dinner and perhaps laugh at some of the funnier moments that had happened to them, both then and now. A few minutes later, Jane's father entered, "there you both are; it is almost seven. Shall we make our way to the dining room?" Tom was starving. He had not eaten much all day; he had been far too busy working to think about food and remembered the only thing Tom had eaten all day was the cake when he first arrived. The three of them walked into the dining room together. Jane was more restrained than before and chose only to walk beside Tom and her father.

Chapter Twenty-Five

Dinner

"Tom, if you would like to sit here to the left of me, Jane can sit to my right," all three of them sat down with lord Sexton sitting at the head of his table. The table was laid out beautifully, with several sets of knives and forks on either side of the plate. Tom once more felt out of place. This was evident to both Jane and her father.

"It's ok, Tom, just start on the outside and work your way in with the flatware," lord Vincent said; this term confused Tom further.

"Daddy means the knives and forks, he rather likes the term flatware." Jane said, smiling away and hoping that Tom was not too stressed or made to feel disagreeable by the situation. Tom understood that this was not his world, so feeling like he was a fish out of water when visiting here he always knew would be inevitable.

"Lord Sexton, you have a lovely home and beautiful gardens."

"Do you like it, Tom? It has been in the family for many generations, each of us merely custodians, of course, keeping it as best we can for the next."

"That must be a big responsibility on your shoulders or whoever takes over, May I ask a difficult question of you both?"

Tom was keen to use the opportunity to enquire more about lord Vincent's situation. However, he was wary of upsetting Jane further. "It all depends on the question, Tom! Is it a polite dinner question suitable for everyone or perhaps does it pertain more to your case and our situation?" Tom was not entirely sure how to answer him; on the one hand, Tom was used to asking difficult questions, especially when interviewing witnesses or suspects. Still, then, on the other hand, he wanted to tread carefully, he did not want Jane upset or her father to become incensed at his line of questioning. Tom decided to change his question and asked.

"Do you both feel the weight of responsibility with your position and prominence in the community and perhaps wonder if it would be easier to have a simpler life?" Tom hoped this question might sound less confrontational than his original.

"There were times back in London, during the war years, that I might have wished things could be simple. The truth is, I believe that I/we have a privileged position to help and support our community and do what we can."

Tom could tell by Jane's reply that she genuinely believed those words; he knew how hard she had worked during the war years to help others; it was always one of the things he had liked.

Lord Sexton added.

"We can never truly appreciate our position on God's earth, whether great or small unless we look to ourselves to offer a helping hand to others. Just because we have these gifts bestowed upon us does not mean we should hoard our gifts from others." Tom was a little surprised to hear lord Sexton voice his views in such a way. He had always thought the upper classes did not care about everyone else and believed themselves superior; it was refreshing to hear. "You look surprised, Tom!" Lord Sexton continued to speak.

"I know what you are thinking; it's ok; almost everyone thinks the same. To be fair to you, contemporaries and ancestors have traditionally lorded it over others in the past, and no doubt there will be many more who continue to do so. However, the world has changed, and we must also." "That is true," Tom added, I believe the first war did that, and the second war sealed its fate; nothing will ever go back to what it once was, of that, I am very sure." Jane did not comment on the subject; she enjoyed watching Tom talk with a refreshing frankness, a frankness she had sorely missed in recent years. Lord Sexton added, "you recognise that this world has changed and continues to do so; where do you see yourself next year and perhaps five years from now?" Replying with a large smile on his face, Tom said.

"Retired, hopefully; this job is not what it used to be; I don't mind the long hours; I can even cope with the terrible things I have seen people do to each other, I wonder though if it would suit younger men and women rather than the tired, grumpy man I believe I have become." Jane looked at Tom more sympathetically; she knew at least some of what he had gone through during the war.

"What about a career change, Tom; perhaps a warm cosy office, somewhere near home, instead of retirement, perhaps even a pay increase with a few more perks added?"

"Be careful, sir; I might think that is possible."

"Never say never, Tom; I believe life has a way of giving back to those who have dedicated themselves in the pursuit of helping others." Tom thought for a moment; he wondered briefly if Jane's father was hinting at a new career for him in return for his help and sensitive handling of Jane's situation. He quickly dismissed this thought, perhaps believing he was overthinking the conversation.

At that moment, Jane began to speak, "so tell me all about your daughter, I understand she is not well, you must be very worried for her?" Tom smiled, pulled out of his jacket pocket his wallet, which contained a picture of the three of them together, and handed it to Jane. "The three of you look very happy, how old is your daughter?"

"She is six years old," Tom replied. "And she mimics her mother in almost every way. Even keeping me in check," Tom said in a warm voice, the kind of tone that a proud father has when talking about their children, believing them to be perfect in every way. "You are right, though; her health is not good at the moment. Emily is in the Bow Arrow hospital receiving treatment. My wife, Mary, may hopefully be able to visit her tomorrow to check on her. I should be able to get a full report then." Tom realised at that moment he sounded very much like a police officer, but it was too late; he had said them that way, and he could not take the words back. To try and soften them, he asked Jane, "Do you have any children?"

Jane went silent for a moment and, trying to find the right words, replied, "I lost my first child; he had poor health when he was born. However, I have been blessed with another boy, also Six years old. It would seem we both have a child of the same age." "Is he here with you? I would love to meet him?" Tom was surprised to hear that Jane had a child; she had not mentioned him before. "No, he is away at boarding school. My husband believes that is the best place for him," Jane replied, looking a little disappointed at not being able to present him to Tom. Tom did not comment on boarding schools. He knew that the upper classes often prefered this way of education. The surprising statement was from lord Sexton, "Well, my dear, perhaps when this is all over, that may change, and we can all be together in the one house." Lord Sexton kept surprising Tom that evening with his modern and progressive thinking; maybe he would have to re-evaluate his views on things a little more.

Dinner lasted approximately two hours. Tom was unsure if that was usual or because he and lord Sexton were constantly evaluating each other with questions and viewpoints. The whole time Jane either looked on admiringly at the both of them or added to the conversation when appropriate questions on Tom's new life since they last met. Either way, Tom enjoyed the evening, the dinner for him was like dining at a fine restaurant, although that was not somewhere he would choose to go. "I think Tom, we should retire to my study for some brandy and discuss our plans to move forward; Jane, would you please excuse us? Maybe you and Tom could catch up some over breakfast." The time of the evening came that Jane was secretly dreading. She wanted to be part of this conversation, even if it was to spend more time with Tom. Jane knew, of course, that Daddy almost certainly had her best interests at heart. Perhaps the conversation may not always be to her liking, so bidding Tom and her father goodnight, she graciously left the room and headed towards her room.

"That was a splendid meal Lord Sexton, thank you." Tom Decided not to allow there to be an awkward silence as they also departed the Dinning room and headed for the study. "Thank you, Tom, you are very gracious. For the rest of the evening and in private, please call me John. I believe we know each other well enough and have each other's best interest at heart." This was a real turning point for Tom; he had not expected to be able to call lord Sexton by his first name, "whatever next", he thought to himself. "I have a very personal question for you, Tom, regarding my daughter," Tom felt he had just been put at ease, and then the rug had been pulled out from underneath him. "Go on," he said gingerly, "ask away," Tom replied, trying not to look affected by this situation. "Regarding my daughter, what was your true relationship back in the day?" Tom knew John would ask something like this but hoped it would never happen.

"Your daughter is a remarkable woman. Her kindness and gentle nature captured my heart in those days. It was only when we had spent a lot of time together during the war years that I learned she was truly a lady of position, but by then, I had already lost my heart to her. Her beauty was not limited to just what I could see on the outside. That was obvious to anyone who stopped to look. She has an inner beauty that shines brighter than any star. I know that nobody is perfect, but that is just how she was for me at that time." Tom paused and gave out a small sigh.

"So if that was the case, why did you not ask her to marry you? I am sure she would have agreed; things could have been very different for you and her."

"That is true; hindsight will always give us a different perspective. Perhaps though, everything said and done, I was a coward and lacked the fortitude needed. However, looking back, I believe that deep down, I knew she was out of my league and destined for bigger things. The life she had here in Scotland, her title and position, none of this was ever a part of my world and nor could it be. I am just a simple copper with a simple life; don't get me wrong, I am very grateful to call her my friend, and for the time we spent together, that will always have a place in my heart." Tom had never really spoken to anyone before about those times with Jane. Although he was a little uncomfortable speaking now, he could confide in John just enough to let him know the kind of person he is. John Listened to all that Tom had said. Tom poured a glass of brandy and handed it to him.

"Thank you, Tom, for your candidness. Jane did speak of you very highly back then and still does today. You know, as I said earlier, if you had asked her, she would have stayed with you. She does not care about money or position, to her people and their character are more important, that is why you are here today and not a private detective or someone who owes me a favour from London. For what it is worth, knowing you now a little better, I would be proud to call you my son in law." Tom appreciated the position he found himself in and felt the playing field had been levelled for them both.

"Thank you, John, Those words were not what I had expected to hear tonight, in fact ever; that means a lot."

"Moving forward," Tom added, hoping to change the conversation to the matter at hand, "I do have some questions I need to ask, which are delicate but important."

"Yes, I believe one of which you were going to ask at dinner but changed your mind after my rebuke." Tom looked directly at John. "Yes, that question, lord Vincent has money troubles. If he loses the dangerous game, he is playing, and we arrest him and further still if we charge him, what happens to his assets such as the house, land and even his title?" "That is an interesting question. Does it have a bearing on your case?"

"Yes, it does; if he loses everything, I need to know how hard he will fight for it all. Would he become dangerous towards Jane or their son? Also, and I am sorry to ask this, will his financial downfall affect you in any way, for the betterment or detriment?" Tom needed to put his detective hat back on, so to speak and ask the difficult questions.

"Well, first of all, Vincents estate, and by this, I mean the house and land, has already remortgaged through a private equity company. I purchased it all almost three weeks ago, so it will not affect Jane or their son, and they will retain their title. He, of course, is unaware of this, as is Jane; this is strictly between us. As to how hard he will fight, I believe he is a nasty man and capable of anything; his business dealings have been unorthodox for some time. There is something you very much need to know; your being here is not by mere coincidence or just at the request of Jane and her letter, which I encouraged her to write. I needed a valid reason for you to be here in this house so that we could talk and quite frankly get the measure of you and the sort of man you are, so the letter from Jane seemed to be the best plan. In the meantime, I asked your chief, as you like to call him. To insist that you be transferred here as soon as possible to work on the two girls' suspicious deaths. I also believe that one of your colleagues, Bob, is very much involved."

Tom listened intently to what John was telling him. He had felt partly used by everyone involved at this point, except Jane. Of course, she had been used by her father to bring him into the house and help her and her father to have a plausible reason for him being here. Tom only spoke to ask further questions, "Why do you believe Bob is involved?" Nothing seemed to shock him anymore about this case, even though he, just a short while ago, believed only himself, George and Rabi, knew of Bob's corrupt ways.

"Tom, you can not easily become a member of the club in question, you have to have and I am ashamed to say, you have to have money, power and position. The original charter for this club was that if you had these three things you could use it for the betterment of others, perhaps raise money for worthy causes, build hospitals, and help orphaned children, that sort of thing. Bob, your colleague could never hope to be a member and yet, somehow he has passed the first stage of membership."

John was getting angrier as he spoke, which Tom could see. "I have to ask this," Tom said, trying to qualify his question.

"If lord Vincent is the chairperson, it is obvious who is supporting Bob; perhaps, he is using it as a carrot to get something else from Bob first, could it be that Bob needs a second supporter, someone such as my chief, after all, he is a long-standing member?"

John thought for a moment and replied, "No!, I am convinced he is not involved; he is a forthright man and would not stand for anything like that." Tom knew his boss was innocent but had to corroborate his theory. It has long been said that in any investigation, you should follow your ABCs, Ask questions, Believe nothing and Check everything. The downside to having that instilled in you is you can become very cynical towards everything and everyone. "That is good to hear, John. I would hate to arrest two officers in one day for obstruction, especially a senior officer of his rank. That is never good for morale, or the reputation of the force, wherever we serve."

"Do you have enough to arrest Bob or Vincent?" John asked, calling him lord stuck in John's throat, "he does not deserve any kind of title in my opinion, well except convict that is." He added.

Tom agreed with John's sentiment in this regard.

"If you ask me, John. Anyone with a position of power or influence should only ever use it to help others, not feather their own nest further."

Tom was rapidly putting all the puzzle pieces together in his mind. He was still a little weary of John. After all, they had only met that day for the first time. Still, after everything was said and done, he knew from his investigation and contacts in London that John was always straight about things.

Tom decided to answer John's question by saying.

"I found out this afternoon that Bob is corrupt. I also believe that lord Vincent Is using the offer for advancement to help Bob in his career by using the club membership as the carrot to lure Bob into helping him. I understand lord Vincent is being investigated for fraud and tax evasion, all of which are being investigated by Bob. So we have the connection and possible wrongdoing; however, we still need proof, although I do have enough to bring all this to the chief. If he decides, we can then quietly arrest Bob. I would not want lord Vincent to be made aware of the arrest as I would like to use Bob to get to him."

"That is very interesting, why do you think Bob is looking to the club for advancement, why not just work hard and apply for promotion?"

"I believe Bob was and perhaps still is a good detective, however since his move here to Scotland, the chances of advancement are not the same as back in London, perhaps he feels trapped here because of his guilt over the accident in which his wife was confined to a wheelchair for the rest of her life. He will never be able to return to London with or without her, also and I am not being dismissive, but fraud cases have to be the most boring of cases to investigate."

John smiled "that is very true, however, sadly it is becoming more and more important in this modern world, people from all walks of life think that it is alright to commit fraud and defraud our government from their rightful dues." John continued, "Is it likely that tomorrow the chief will agree with your recommendations?"

"I am sure he will. I need Bob to confess his part in this and implicate or, better still, swear an oath to the fact that lord Vincent is up to his neck in this. I need to get to the bottom of the suspicious deaths and find out exactly what happened and why their bodies were moved, and, for that matter, why make it look similar to the murders from a previous case of mine? All these questions need answering, and the girl's families will want closure."

Tom knew what he had to do tomorrow morning, but before he did all this, he would have to brief his small team first and then the chief. "Ok, Tom, great work; I can see you have a good handle on everything. Will you do me a professional courtesy of letting me know how the case is progressing? My original plan was to present Vincent with enough circumstantial evidence to get him to agree to an uncontested divorce from Jane. This, it would seem, is far bigger and long-reaching; you have to do your job well and get convictions for everyone's sake, I will find another way for Jane. Look it is getting late, we should call it a night, I will not be around in the morning to have breakfast with you and Jane, I have to return to London early, I am sure you understand, the pressure of responsibility and work."

"Of course John, thank you for the information and also thank you for your hospitality, it has been a most interesting evening; I am just sorry that we have had to meet under these circumstances and my heart does genuinely go out to Jane and her son, this must be very difficult for everyone."

"Thank you, Tom, you are a good man; I can see why Jane liked you so much and trusted in you. I am sure your career has a lot further to go before you retire." Tom was not sure what to make of John's final remark. Could he be hinting again at a promotion when all this is over? after quickly mulling it over in his head Tom dismissed the idea. He had already decided to retire when this was all over. Tom knew now more than ever that being with his family was more important than anything else, so he graciously and polity replied, "Thank you."

Chapter Twenty-Six

The morning after

Tom was still up early. Although Tom had gone to bed late that night, he continued mulling over all the events and conversations of the day in his mind. The idea of seeing Jane that morning to talk freely was very alluring to him. Finally, he had a chance to speak unincumbered.

Tom was aware that Jane may still hold a torch for him, and if he was candid with himself, the idea did appeal to him. However, he wanted to let Jane know just how in love with Mary he was, but he needed to do it subtly. Tom did not want to cause any problems for Jane. He knew she was dealing with many emotions and needed support, not emotional distance from him.

When Tom arrived in the dining room, Jane was already waiting for him. Her intrigue at last night's conversation that she was not a party to had overcome her, "Good morning, Tom, did you sleep well?" Tom looked at Jane; despite all she had gone through and dealt with, she looked as lovely and beguiling as she had always done.

"I did, very much, thank you, it is a lovely room, not what I am used to." Tom had felt he had slept in a high-class hotel and only wished Mary could have been with him. "Mary will be very jealous when I tell her about my room and the big bed." He said to Jane, hoping to instil how much he thought about his wife and loved her.

"I am pleased; maybe you can bring her to visit and stay a few days; I would love to meet the woman who stole your heart and makes you happy."

Jane was trying to be positive and, at the same time, trying hard not to jump into the conversation regarding the late-night discussion with her father. "Come and sit here next to me; I want to hear all about her."

Tom told Jane how he had met her at the cafe across the street from the train station. As requested, he sat down next to her, poured himself a cup of tea and brought him a full-cooked breakfast as one of the maids. Tom was a little confused but thought it was an excellent opportunity.

Jane interrupted him by saying, "Surely not the night, you let me leave on the train for Edinburgh!" The tone of Jane's voice had changed and sounded a mix of surprise and disdain at meeting someone else so soon after her leaving.

"No, of course not, although I did go to the cafe after you left, and surprisingly enough she did serve me that night although I did not remember her, my mind was elsewhere at the time. The queen herself could have served me and would not have noticed that night and I would have not realised. The moment I let you go my heart sank into a deep depression, I could think of nothing else. It was much later when I had to visit the cafe on police business when we met properly."

Tom had not meant to say how awful he had felt about that night to Jane; it just slipped out, almost as if he had to say so, even without his understanding. Jane, on the other hand, was pleased; her tone of voice gave away her feelings at Tom's statement when she replied, "I am so sorry we parted like that, I am sure I was also to blame by not saying how I felt about you." Jane's gracious attitude began to shine again; she continued, "It is rather strange how things turn out, sometimes for the good, in your case and sometimes, well not so good. Don't get me wrong, I was happy for a while after I met my husband and then life and duty take over and before you know it, well, you know the rest." Tom smiled, letting Jane speak.

"On another note, how did your meeting go with daddy last night?" Although he expected Jane to ask him questions about last night's conversation, he was not expecting it right then.

"well, erm, sorry I was deep in thought then at what you said about us and your life with lord Vincent, what was the question you asked?"

Tom thought this delay tactic might help rescue him. However, Jane was not so easily dissuaded from her curiosity. She repeated her question.

"How did your evening go with daddy?"

Tom replied in a rather vague manner, "Not bad, he is a very interesting man, he loves you more than anything or anyone."

"I know," Jane replied, "I was wondering if you both have sorted out a plan to move forward, which will benefit everyone."

Jane had not wanted to sound self-centred, but the thought of not knowing how things would go was eating away inside her. Unlike Tom, she had not slept well that night; her fears were causing nightmares and constantly awakening her.

"Well, we have a positive plan to move forward with my case, and I am, that is to say, your father and I are sure things will be resolved positively for you, of that we are very sure." Tom did not want to say how her father would now have to make alternative plans on Jane's behalf. However, he tried to reassure her that everything would be all right.

"I do have to say though, Jane I can not say the same for your husband lord Vincent, the net is closing in on him and very quickly, I am sorry to say; I do hope you forgive me for that, however, I must do my job, it is important to do that to the best of my ability." Jane smiled and replied," I know Tom, you are a good man of principle and I have always appreciated that. please do not let all of this get in the way of our newfound friendship, I have a feeling you, your family and I can be great friends moving forward."

Tom agreed and said, "Jane, it has been wonderful to catch up after all these years. For now, though, I must thank you for your hospitality and be on my way. I have a very difficult and busy day ahead of me." Jane agreed to let Tom go without more questions but added.

"I have arranged for daddy's car to take you back once you are ready, your bags should be packed and in the car already, thank you for your kind words, and your discretion in all of this." They both smiled at each other as Jane stood, leaned forward and softly kissed Tom on the cheek to say goodbye. Tom was a little taken aback by the gesture from Jane. However, he was not about to show this; Tom took his leave of Jane and headed towards the front door, feeling a little surprised to see Lord Sexton's driver and car waiting for him. Tom believed he would have driven to London to meet Lord Sexton from the train. "Good morning sir, It is good to see you again, shall I drive you to your lodgings first or would you prefer to go directly to the station first?"

The driver seemed pleased to see Tom that morning. The feeling was mutual, although he felt a little uncomfortable having a chauffeur, especially with such a car as a Rolls Royce.

"I am instructed to be at your service today for as long as you need me, sir." The driver said.

"That is very good of lord Sexton. I am sure; if you take me to the station, that will be enough; I would not want people thinking I am acting above my station," Tom said jokingly.

"Lord Sexten did ask me to drive you back today. However, it was Lady Vincent, his daughter, that offered the car to you for the rest of the day." Tom did not know what to make of this. However, he still chose not to keep the car or the driver's services. Instead, he asked to pass on his sincere thanks to her ladyship.

"And also, may I say thank you to you for your services and to the other members of the household team; everything was wonderful, thank you." After Tom said those words, he replayed the sentence in his mind and thought, "That sounded as if I am so superior to everyone; I hope it was not taken that way."

"That's ok, sir; we are happy to serve, especially when it is someone like yourself. Someone who is hardworking and trying to protect us from terrible people who kill and the such."

"That is very kind of you; I am just doing my duty."

"I know, sir, just like us, except yours has more danger." Tom laughed a little; he had not expected to have such a conversation this morning; it was fascinating.

"May I ask you another question?" Tom asked politely, "yes, sir, if you wish," Tom continued by asking, "your accent is English; how is that you come to work here?"

"Ah! you spotted that, sir. No wonder you're a great detective."

The chauffeur said with a rye smile and a little cheekiness."

Tom laughed a little louder and replied, "yes, years of training gave me that edge; you know we go to a special school to learn accents."

The banter had become a little more fun; the chauffeur continued by saying, "Both my parents are indeed Scottish, however, I was raised in London, you see they both served lord Sexton's parents at their London address, so naturally, eventually I joined them as a driver."

Tom found this quite fascinating and probed a little further, "and do all drivers for these types of families all start the same way, with their family serving first?"

"Not always, sir, however, many do, it is a very trusted position, it is certainly the same for lady Vincent's husband, his driver's family go back at least three generations."

"Wow, you certainly learn something new every day, I say, so if I retire it is unlikely I could get a job as a driver then for a well-to-do family?"

"I am afraid so, sir, these sort of jobs rarely become available as discretion is often required, so the families prefer someone they have known for a long time."

"O well, maybe I will continue doing what I, allegedly am good at." They both laughed a little more.

"Here we go sir, If you like I can take your luggage back to your bed and breakfast, it is no trouble." Tom liked this man more; as the conversation continued, it was a shame he thought it would have to end so quickly.

"That would be wonderful, if you are sure that you don't mind, it would be a big help and of course, and stop some of the questions as to where I have been all night."

"You see sir, discretion is often required. Yes, I am happy to do this for you; I only ask you that you look after the family as best you can, given the circumstances." Tom, perhaps would have been a little surprised by that comment before today, as it signalled to him that he knew some of what was going on but was not prepared to say any more.

"I will certainly try, sir; you take care, yourself."

"Of course, I will do my level best. Lord Sexton and his daughter are good people; that is very clear to see. Oh and don't worry about getting the door, I can do that. Thank you, enjoy the rest of your day."

Tom headed into the station; he was sure everyone was looking at him as he did. Very few coppers get chauffeured to work in the morning in such a lovely car; I could get used to that, he chuckled. As Tom turned the corner to head for his murder room come office, he bumped straight into George and Rabi, who were standing there holding some tea and searching their pockets for the keys to the room.

"Morning, gentleman," Tom said, almost knocking into them.

"We have a big day ahead of ourselves," before he could say any more, George asked Tom, "since you have a new driver and car does this mean Rabi is now out of work sir?"

George and Rabi had seen the car pull up and let Tom out.

"It is amazing what perks can come your way, boys, when you're a world-famous detective, solving crime in two different countries." Tom had never really believed this himself but thought it might be funny enough to make the boys laugh and not press the question further.

This had seemed to work until they all entered the room when Rabi pushed a little more.

"So, sir, why did you get a lift to work in such a nice car this morning?" Tom had not wanted to answer that question so directly, so he let Rabi's question hang for a moment. Enough time passed for George to jump in again.

"Well, sir, we understand if you do not want to tell us. You should remember, though, that you have taught us to ask difficult questions and not just accept the first answer, so you see, you only have yourself to blame for our questions."

Rabi thought George might have gone too far and nudged him with his elbow. Tom laughed. Well, it is good to see you are both learning. Tom had overcome the question so far and knew they might ask again as they were highly qualitative about such things. Well done; let's sit down and discuss what we are doing today. Still,

I need to brief you on some serious aspects of this case, which have far broader implications than we had first realised.

Tom went on to tell them that they would likely be making an arrest today. "This won't be pleasant for anyone, and you need to be aware, though, that when this happens, you will have the full backing of the chief and me. Whatever happens, you have proved your selves to be exemplary officers of the law. At this stage, however, I cannot say who we will arrest or when this happens. I will have to first brief the chief on the whole matter and decide how to best handle it. I will call you both into the office once I have done this."

George and Rabi, at first, looked excited at the thought of arresting someone. Still, they became more concerned when they learned it might have further implications.

"What do you mean by implications to us, and who might we be arrested today? Is it the murderer?"

Tom looked at them more kindly and replied, "As I said earlier, I need to protect you both, and no, it is not the murderer. However, I can say it is someone connected to our case in more ways than one. We cannot afford to make any mistakes at this stage, so please, for now, no more questions. In the meantime, I need you both to run some errands to keep you out of harm's way; they are essential and will not take you too long. I want you both to take an unmarked car and go and see if lord Vincent's driver is at the house, do not let him know you are there. Secondly, I need you to double-check that lord Vincent was at the party on the night in question and how long he stayed. When you get back, please come straight to the chief's office, knock twice to let me know you are here and wait outside. Can you do that?

"Yes sir, we can." George and Rabi were both in agreement.

"One more thing, did you get a copy of the visitor's logs for the cells?"

"Yes sir, they are here on your desk ready for you."

"Excellent work chaps, I will see you very soon all being well."

Tom left the room, leaving Rabi and George to lock up and headed to the chief's office.

Chapter Twenty-Seven

Briefing the chief

Tom arrived at the chief's office, knocked on the door and waited to be beckoned rather than walking in.

"Come in!"

"Morning sir," Tom said, hoping to keep himself calm before the inevitable storm that would ensue before the day's end.

"Yes, good morning, Tom. Was that lord Sexton's car and driver I saw dropping you off this morning?"

Nothing could escape the chief, or it would seem anyone else at the station. "Yes, sir, you have a keen eye," Tom said, hoping to keep the mood light.

"Hmm, yes, it would appear; I have not lost it yet, Tom. Can you tell me why?" The chief was pushing hard for the information and, judging by the tone of his voice, was more severe than Tom had realised at first. "Well, sir, It is all connected to this case, which is why I am here; I need to give you the full picture now, and it is not a nice one." Tom hesitated very briefly before continuing.

"We have a dirty police officer in our midst who is compromising his case against a peer of the realm in favour of advancement and maybe financial gain for himself. "That is a serious statement to make. Do you have any proof?" The chief raised his voice slightly before calming down to hear the rest of what Tom had to say. "That is why lord Sexton's driver dropped me off, you see. I believe I mentioned yesterday that I know his daughter from about ten years ago. When I worked on another case, we all presumed it to be similar or the same as this one. Of course, I can prove it is not the same murderer."

The chief sat down at his desk; he knew this would be a long story; Tom followed suit and continued his explanation. "The way I understand all of this, he asked you to request my presence on this case; it seemed he knew my reputation from before. He informed me that a fellow police officer has already passed the first stage of joining this club of yours, a club that, in other circumstances, he could never hope to be involved in, due to the exclusive entrance scrutiny. This was first brought to our attention by James, the man I arrested previously and charged with assault, conspiracy to pervert the course of justice, Dealing of class A drugs and providing young girls for the express purpose of prostitution. There are more charges pending, sir, on him; however, he has been very helpful in pointing us in the right direction towards both lord Vincent and our dirty police officer. On that note sir, the officer in question has for no apparent reason been in to see James, and I believe he is trying to intimidate him into not giving us an accurate statement and taking the fall for everything. "

"I believe if we arrest the officer now and quietly, we can avoid a lot of repercussions. If we play it just right, I should be able to use him to turn on lord Vincent. While I'm thinking about it, my officers Rabi and George have proved to be excellent officers. Fearless when required, steadfast in their duties and I believe they will go on to make great detectives one day given the opportunity for promotion sir, which of course is entirely your decision. I would like it on record, their hard work and tenacity have played a big part in the breaking of this case. In fact, sir, right now they are checking that both, lord Vincent and his driver are at home. Lord Vincents driver may prove to be of great use to us if we can get him to talk."

"Just why do you think the driver will be of help, Tom?"

"Well, sir, as I was being driven to the station by lord Sexton's driver, we had an interesting chat. It would appear that Vincent's driver has been with the family many years, and drivers often know things that perhaps others should not, especially things like where their masters are, who may have been in the vehicles and of course, they are often party to conversations that require a great deal of discretion."

"Well, Tom, you have certainly been doing your job; I will take on board your thoughts on your two officers and see what I can do for them. right now, though, you have not told me who the officer in question is that you believe is corrupt; who is it?" As if choreographed, but very much on queue, two knocks came on the door.

"Right on time sir, my two officers, they should be in this room for the rest of what I have to say, after all, they will have to play another big part in what happens next."

"Very well then Tom, let them in."

Tom opened the door, and both Rabi and George entered; they looked and felt awkward as they were unsure what would happen next.

The chief then spoke to them, saying. "Tom here tells me that you have proved yourselves to be excellent officers and have carried out your duties in a way that would make this station and the force proud. The duty you perform today and how you handle it will always be a matter of record. I want you to know that we will soon be making an arrest which, from what I have just been told, will bring repercussions to us all. So I want you to know this, stand firm, be strong and always act in a manner that is becoming an officer of the law, and you will always have my support, gentleman."

This speech surprised everyone in the room; both Rabi and George felt proud at this moment and ready to conquer Everest if that was required of them.

"Now Tom, may we all know who is being arrested today?" The chief asked after his almost vitriolic speech that perhaps sounded more like Churchill himself.

"Yes, of course, Sir, It is Bob in the fraud department. He is supposed to be as you know, working on the fraud case against lord Vincent. However, Vincent has seduced Bob with the offer of advancement through the club which would in, turn, put him higher on your radar in the hope of promotion. Which I might add at this point, I know you would never do sir."

"I should hope so, Tom. You know after Bob's arrest, it will not be easy for any of us. It could also tip off lord Vincent, especially if he is involved in this whole sorry mess. Whilst we are on the subject of lord Vincent do you think he killed those two girls?"

Tom reached into his briefcase and pulled out the girls' autopsy reports. "Here is the thing, both girls it would appear were not murdered at all; they both died from drug overdoses."

"But what about the hand prints and the bruising around their necks, were they not strangled to death?"

"At first, sir, we thought that strangulation was the cause of death, however, after the autopsy report, it appears not to be the case."

"So what about the bruising on both girls necks?"

"It would appear, sir, that the bruising occurred soon after death; designed to throw us all of course."

"So please tell me, we can prove Vincent gave the drugs to the girls!"

"Sadly not, sir; the drugs were brought to the party by the girls; given to them by James, who we have in custody."

The chief did not look happy at this turn of events.

"If Vincent, did not supply or handle the drugs and the girls died from an overdose, then what do we have on Vincent?"

"Well, to start, sir, first we have him on bribery of a police officer, and I'm hoping to get him on two accounts of perverting the course of justice. The first account is his fraud case, second, inciting the illegal moving and disposing of two dead bodies and all this along with conspiracy. If all goes well with Bob's arrest, we can add further charges later."

"That's something, but I don't like the if's, there Tom. Are you sure you can do this?"

"This is why I need Rabi to go and ask Bob to come to your office saying you need his help on a delicate matter. I am sorry to say Rabi but you always look the most innocent, it is a gift I assure you."

Rabi was not sure what to make of this.

"George, I need you to stay here; please just wait in the corner of the room for me to make the arrest, then cuff him, and we will then sit him down together. This should be the best way to reduce any talk from his colleagues and hopefully not tip off lord Vincent either. We do not know if others are involved in his team; of course, that alone will warrant a full internal investigation and perhaps put other officers under suspicion. These sort of things often unravel very quickly."

Tom did not want to overthink the further ramifications. He knew, well hoped anyway, that he would be back in London for this part, having said that he did not wish this kind of trouble on any station or police force.

"Sir, I believe we should do this now before the day goes on; I am reliably informed that Bob is in his office until midday, when he leaves for lunch and who knows what!" Tom spoke more determinedly, adding confidence to the situation, which he knew would help his two constables.

"OK, let's go ahead, Rabi; you know what to do, yes?"

Rabi nodded and confirmed what he would only say. "The chief wants to see him in his office to help him with a delicate matter as soon as possible."

Tom nodded in approval. The chief added. "Well done, Rabi, keep it simple, and do not elaborate; if he asks what is it about? just say something, like I am only a constable, sir, then bring him to me."

"Yes, sir, shall I go now?" Rabi asked to make sure.

Tom replied, yes, Rabi go ahead, well done." George also nodded with approval as Rabi left the room.

Rabi felt nervous inside but was determined not to let it show. He had a responsible job to carry out. So he tried to remind himself that a criminal is still a criminal, even if they pretend to be police officers or start with good intentions.

It was not long before Rabi arrived at Bob's office; as he looked through the small glass window, he could see three other officers working hard at their desks. At the back of the room, he could see Bob in his small office. Rabi's heart began to beat faster, with his breath becoming shorter. To calm himself down, he told himself that "at least he was not arresting Bob in front of everyone on his own." Rabi girded himself with this thought and entered the office area, heading directly to where Bob was sitting. "Excuse me, constable, can I help you?" came a voice from the first desk as he passed it.

"I have a message from the chief for Bob, I mean the detective." In all the excitement, Rabi had forgotten Bob's last name; he began to feel embarrassed at this; thankfully, Bob heard and gestured to him that he could come over.

"You have a message for me from the chief?" He asked, almost looking smug.

"Yes sir, he asked if you could come to his office as soon as possible to help him with a rather delicate matter."

Rabi replied softer, not letting anyone else hear what he had to say.

Bob believed this was his chance, the reward for helping lord Vincent; his smugness grew larger than previously. "Lead on then, constable."

Bob said out loud, then added so that the rest of the room could hear. "I am off to the chief's office; I may well be some time; please hold all my calls and take any messages for me, and I should not be disturbed."

Rabi could not believe what he was hearing and seeing. Bob's arrogance seemed to know no bounds; if only he could arrest him now, he thought, that would wipe the smile off his face. Rabi no longer felt intimidated by Bob or the situation; he was almost looking forward to what would happen next. Bob never asked further questions about the situation, preferring to believe that lord Vincent had come through for him. They soon reached the chief's office, and after knocking and receiving the usual, "come in," Rabi walked in first and announced that Bob was here as requested.

Bob walked into the room, unaware that he was walking into an ambush; Rabi closed the door and stood directly in front of it to prevent anyone from entering the office by mistake. "Sir, you wanted to see me," Bob said, looking pleased with himself; at that moment, he noticed Tom standing behind him.

"Hello Tom, I did not see you there, how are you? How is the case going?" Bob was still full of himself. The chief stood there and said nothing in reply. Then without notice, Tom stepped forward and spoke.

"Detective Robert Jenkins, I am arresting you on suspicion of perverting the course of justice. Intimidating a witness and taking bribes to knowingly cover the crimes in which two young girls were found dead."

The room was silent; you could hear a pin drop. The chief then broke the silence and said, "This is a dark day, Bob, not just for you but for all of us, for the force and for your family, words will never truly say how we all feel about this moment, the shame you have brought upon us all must and will be your burden alone." With that, George stepped forward and placed the handcuffs on Bob, then sat him down in front of the chief.

Chapter Twenty-Eight

The arrest

B ob could not believe what had just happened. One minute, he was expecting great things. The next minute, his world had been crashed down around him by Tom, the man he had once called a friend and only a few days earlier had around his house to enjoy a meal with him and his wife. The sickening feeling in the depths of his bowls almost caused them to open if it were not for the same sense in his stomach. Both feelings simultaneously brought him to the point of gaging on his vomit. Bob was not a hardened criminal, which made this all the harder for everyone in the room. Putting his hand on Bob's shoulder, Tom said in a measure of kindness, "Bob, what happened to you? You are or were a good copper and an outstanding detective. When we last worked together, you were very accommodating and keen to do well, like my two constables here, George and Rabi." Both George and Rabi were still shocked at how Bob must have changed so much from being like them to the man they now saw sitting in front of them. Both of them looked at each other silently. They both made a pact never to let themselves become like Bob. Everyone could see that Bob was great full for the sentiment from Tom. Tom pulled his chair to align it with the chief so that both could now face Bob directly.

Bob stayed silent for some time; he was not a stupid man; he knew what would happen. So the whole time, Bob kept replaying different ideas in his head. Some would be to confess everything and hope for mercy; others were based on lord Vincent stepping in as if somehow, he had the influence to do so.

"Never in all my years here on the force have I felt such regret allowing an officer of the law transfer into my station. As far as I am concerned, you deserve everything that happens next, but for now, I must advise you of your rights; Constable Rabi, would you please do this? Rabi did just as the chief requested. When he had finished, the chief then told George and Rabi.

"Take him to the cells, and tell the desk sergeant not to allow anyone except either of you in. In fact, second thoughts, I would like both of you to stay there until Tom arrives to take a formal statement. I am sorry to say this will be a long day for everyone."

It was hard for George and Rabi to work out what the chief thought after he made that statement; however, they knew what their duty was, so both of them stood up and helped Bob to his feet. The chief added.

"Of course, you can waive your rights, and make a full and frank statement now!" Tom looked a bit surprised at the chief making that kind of offer. However, he was not about to contradict him. Tom signalled to George and Rabi to wait just a moment before leading him off; the chief continued.

"Well what do you say, Bob?" Bob barely said a word except to say, "No thank you." The chief stared at Bob with great disappointment, shook his head in disbelief and signalled to the two constables to carry on.

As George and Rabi led Bob in handcuffs away, they both felt a real sense of pressure. It felt so wrong, especially as Bob was a senior officer. Added to this, they were convinced every police officer in the station was now coming out to see them. This was not the case; they had only seen a couple of other officers; they just stopped, stood to one side and looked down to the floor. They had known Bob, which was shameful to everyone on the force. They soon arrived at the cells and presented Bob to the custody sergeant.

The sergeant looked surprised to see Bob in cuffs and initially said, "very funny, constables, the joke is over, back to work." Bob looked at him, and immediately the sergeant knew this was no joke, "what are the charges?" he asked.

George and Rabi looked at him, and one of them replied. "Sir, this is a request from the chief and inspector Richards. Could you please phone his office for the charges? They have requested we stay with you and not let anyone enter his cell for any reason except for the inspector or the chief himself." The custody sergeant had never heard of anything like this before, so picking up the phone, he did as requested and confirmed the situation; "Yes sir, absolutely sir, right away." He put the phone down and now looked more concerned than ever. "Ok, chaps, this is how we are going to proceed. First, check the prisoner for sharp objects, remove laces from his shoes, and take off his tie; whilst I process him. Any valuables will need to be placed into this tray to be verified, counted and documented; Bob, I mean, sir. I need to ask you to sign here; at this point, we usually take fingerprints. However, his should be on file." The custody sergeant tried hard to carry on as he usually did, but this proved difficult. "Should we not do that anyway? We do not want the chief or the inspector saying we cut corners or gave any special treatment to him on account of his, well, what I mean to say who he is?" Rabi did not want to cause problems by contradicting the sergeant. However, he felt after all that had happened, we all needed to follow procedures as we usually would in any other case. "You're right, constable; well done; let's get this done right for everyone's sake."

By now, rumours were spreading fast around the station, and it seemed as though officers were finding some very tenuous reason to see if the stories were true. Bob was quickly processed and allowed to make his one phone call. Everyone assumed it would be to his solicitor as usual in these circumstances. Bob never said; either way, it was short and to the point; Bob was then taken to his cell and the handcuffs removed. When the heavy metal door closed behind him, Bob turned to see that George had unlocked the viewing portal to see what Bob would do. Bob stared back for a few seconds, then turned away and walked over to the hard concrete raised slab. On top sat a thin, heavy plastic-coated mattress and a simple pillow with a grey blanket. George continued watching for several minutes before replacing the flap and returning to his colleagues at the desk. "I can't help but wonder," George began saying. "that we should continue to monitor him whilst we wait for his solicitor to arrive. I have a feeling looking at him that he might try something stupid." George felt very strongly about this, so he and Rabi agreed they would take turns checking in on him every ten minutes. The custody sergeant agreed, saying, "we have never lost anyone yet, but you are right. We have never had an officer of the law in custody, charged with such crimes either."

Bob sat down on his new concrete bed and held his head in his hands, "I have been a fool," he thought to himself. "What am I going to do about this? What evidence do they have on me?" Questions flooded his head as he tried to justify his actions in his mind. All the time, he was trying out more lies and excuses to see if they sounded plausible or not. Bob had once been a great detective, not a great lier or master criminal. However, he did console himself because he knew the law well and thought he had connections in high places.

After the two constables escorted Bob out of the room to the cells, Tom turned to the chief and said. "Well, under the circumstances, at least this part of the plan has gone smoothly. What are your thoughts, chief?"

The chief took a deep breath, just as Tom often did before making difficult decisions. He looked at Tom and replied. "This is a bleak day for us, Tom. It will blacken the reputation of this station for a long time to come, not to mention that it will jeopardise any convictions Bob had secured in recent years. This really is a terrible day."

Tom allowed the chief to talk before trying to be more positive.

"Sir, you are right, of course, but now at least we can clean house, and hopefully, if I do my job right, get a conviction against lord Vincent for the wrongful deaths of those girls. Looking at Bob sitting there, I have a strong feeling that he already knows it would be best to cooperate with us and turn him to state evidence. Especially if we can offer a deal on his sentence; I am not a fan of that normally; however, in this instance, it could prove useful."

The chief thought for a few moments and agreed, "don't offer anything concrete lay out the evidence and tempt him in to see if he bites, the same way we fly fish, have you ever tried it, Tom, there are some excellent trout fishing here."

"No sir, I'm not really a fisherman, however, I do get the metaphor and have tried similar many times."

Tom and the chief continued chatting for some time about the case when the chief suddenly looked at Tom and smiled, saying. "I once heard that the mark of an admirable man is his steadfastness in the face of trouble, Tom; you have proved to be an admirable man."

Tom was unsure how to reply to that; he did not expect such praise from the chief, especially as the case was not entirely over. Instead, Tom replied, "ah, Beethoven, I believe, sir, high praise indeed; perhaps we should wait to see how this turns out first before I accept any praise."

"Perhaps you're right Tom, however, you have proved yourself here in Scotland, we would be happy to keep you here, if you wish, perhaps I might even teach you to fish."

Tom smiled and said, "I believe sir, I should make a start on securing our next arrest first if you would excuse me."

"Of course, Tom, go ahead, get something we can all be proud of."

Tom Left the room and headed to the canteen first; he knew his lads would need some refreshment after their stressful day. He thought *It should be a pint*; however, the day was far from over, and it felt inappropriate to celebrate this win.

Chapter Twenty-Nine

Planting trees

Tom arrived at the cells and the custody desk with four cups of tea, not including his own; one for each officer and the fourth for Bob. "How are you all doing?" He asked them. The officers looked at Tom, not knowing what to say in return, Tom added. "It is challenging, I know. I'm sure, like the rest of us, you may be feeling numb right now, but things will get better. We have a long road ahead of us, and we can get through this if we work together; for now, though I would like to see our prisoner, I will also need one of you with me, Rabi, I think you. "Rabi was surprised by this but was more than happy to watch and learn.

Tom entered the cell and said, "Bob, I've brought you a cuppa, I'm sure you could do with one after all that you have been through." Tom handed him the tea and added, "you cannot say a word until your solicitor or union rep is here, however you can listen, I have one simple question for you to think about until I return; when is the best time to plant a tree?" Rabi looked very confused, "Was this some sort of code Tom was using to communicate secretly with Bob?" He thought to himself. Tom then stood up and beckoned Rabi, and then they both left the room.

Looking confused, Rabi asked Tom. "What was that all about, sir? Was it some of that cockney rhyming slang I have heard about?" "No Rabi, it was more to do with another case which Bob worked on many years ago; I wanted to jog his memory a little and get him onside."

Rabi was still confused and could not understand why this was all Tom had to say to Bob. He pushed a little tougher in his questions. "How does that get him on your side? I'm confused?"

Both George and the custody sergeant were now interested in this conversation. They stopped what they were doing to hear what Tom had to say.

"It was Bob's first case when he took the lead as a detective with me as his mentor; there had been a murder in a place in London known as china town, Bob was given some advice by a woman who was known in the community for her wisdom, and was very well respected by all who lived there. Early on in the investigation, she gave Bob some of her wisdom to help him solve the case, she asked him when is the best time to plant a tree, if he could answer correctly she would help him further as it would show he is a deep thinker and not someone who would act disrespectfully towards her way of life."

George asked inquisitively, "what is the answer?"

Tom replied, "that is the question, perhaps you should think about it as well, if things go well when his solicitor arrives the answer will reveal itself, talking about solicitors, when is his due to arrive, I need to get started?"

The custody sergeant spoke up and said, "we are not sure sir, however, the duty solicitor is here if that helps?"

"Strange, but ok, give it another ten minutes; if one doesn't come, send in the duty solicitor, we can't wait forever." Moments later, a solicitor walked in and said. "My name is Catherine Mcewen; here's my card; I am the appointed solicitor for Bob Jenkins; I believe you have him in custody." Tom stepped forward and replied, "Yes, I am the arresting officer. Mr Jenkings is in cell two; I have seen to it he is comfortable and personally taken him a cup of tea. He has been cautioned, and I am now waiting to interview him, and I have to say, the case against him is robust. The chief here, and I am sure the chief procurator, will want to prosecute to the full extent of the law. We are not looking to go softly on him just because he was a serving police officer." Catherine looked at Tom, and at that moment, Tom could see she was not a battle-hardened solicitor with years of experience.

Tom knew he could exploit this; he had seen people like her many times before.

"Well, sir," she replied, that may well be the case. However, I need some time alone with my client before you start your interview process. So if you could be so kind as to have one of your constables show me to an interview room and bring my client to me, that would be a good start." Catherine was not naive. She had some experience. However, she was newly qualified but was determined not to let it show, or so she thought.

Bob was taken from his cell and led to the interview room where Catherine, his solicitor, was waiting for him. "Hello Bob, my name is Catherine. I am here to look after your interests and see what we can do to help you. First of all, how are you? have they been treating you well? And more importantly, have they tried to interview you yet or ask any questions?" Bob looked pleased to see a friendly face in all of this and replied, "I'm good, thanks, and no, they have not asked me anything yet." "That is good to hear, Bob. Now, I have the charge sheet in front of me, and as I am sure you are aware, these are some very serious charges against you. Having spoken to the arresting officer outside, it looks as though they are going to try and make an example of you."

Bob knew this would probably be the case in his heart, "dirty coppers leave a bad stench in a nick," he thought to himself. "What do you advise then, Catherine?" Bob asked. "I am not interested in whether or not you are guilty of any of these charges, my job here really is to minimise, control and get you the best possible outcome. Suppose I can exonerate you at the same time. In that case, we may even get your job back, or we can claim constructive dismissal and perhaps get you a healthy compensation as the job could become untenable for you. Before we can do any of that though, we will need to see what evidence they have against you and why they believe you are corrupt. So for any question they ask, I want you to only reply, no comment." Bob liked the sound of all of this, especially the compensation. However, in his heart, he knew this could never happen; Tom was too much of a great detective and very thorough; he had proved this by the way he was arrested. Catherine opened the interview room door and spoke to Rabi, who had been standing guard outside. "Will you please inform the arresting officer we are ready and waiting for him?"

Tom had been busying himself in his murder room, collating paperwork and planning his next step. He knew he wanted to make an example of Bob to show everyone that all crimes would be prosecuted fully without exception, even so-called police officers. Rabi arrived, "Sir, it would appear. They are ready for you; can I and George be present for the interview?" he asked. Tom replied, "yes of course one of you can sit beside me. The other will have to stand in the corner by the door, and you must keep silent, use the experience to learn, and I am sure I do not have to say it, do not speak about it with anyone else." Tom was very firm when speaking; everything had to be played just right for his plan to come to fruition.

They all entered the interview room, each person taking their position without a word. Tom then made his introductions and confirmed who else was present, "How are you, Bob? Do you need anything before we start?" Tom recognised that Bob was no ordinary criminal; he was not like the others they had both known over the years. Bob knew how Tom interviewed people. He had been with him plenty of times before. He had also employed many of his tricks and ways, so Bob politely smiled and, as instructed, he did not make a reply verbally.

Tom continued to speak, setting out all the evidence he had, "look Bob, out of respect for you and your years of service, I am not going to treat you like any other person I have had sat in front of me, you deserve better than that. I also know that your brief would likely have advised you to make a typical no-comment interview."

Tom looked at Bob's council and added, "would that be right Catherine?"

Catherine was not amused by this tactic and replied, "Inspector Richards, please address all your comments and questions to my client, not me!" Tom had expected Catherine to make such a comment and was not fazed by this.

"Of course, councillor, my apologies. This is what I am going to do. I am going to tell you all that we have on you. As I do, you have the option to ignore your solicitor's advice and answer, or you can keep quiet in the misguided hope of beating these charges.

And remember Bob, how many people have sat opposite us and did a no-comment interview. We still got convictions." Catherine tried to interrupt at this point to express her dislike of Tom's attitude. However, Tom shut her down immediately, saying. "Please remember you are here to advise your client, not run my interview, so please keep your comments to yourself and your client, not me!" Tom's tone of voice had turned sterner; George and Rabi had not seen this side of him before.

"Bob, we know in exchange for misleading your fraud case. And losing evidence that might otherwise gain a conviction against lord Vincent. You are being offered a position in a very prestigious club, a club that the likes of you and I, under normal circumstances, could never hope to be a member of due to their extremely high entrance requirements. We know this because we have statements from two long-term club members who are willing to go on record and make sworn oaths to this effect, and yet you have already passed the first stage. Secondly, we have an eyewitness who swears to the fact that you have been seen doing favours of an illegal nature for lord Vincent. Our witness also has sworn that you have received large amounts of cash for your services. Added to all of this, Bob, according to our entry logs. You had visited my prisoner, without due reason, early hours of the morning when you were not officially on duty. Our prisoner also claims you have used your position to intimidate him into not cooperating with us. In return, lord Vincent will look after him financially and protect him whilst in prison." Tom paused for a few minutes to let this all sink in before continuing, "So Bob, my only question is this, when is the best time to plant a tree?" Tom stopped talking again, looked directly at Bob and waited for the reply. Bob did not say a word to anyone except his solicitor in an undertone so that no one else could hear. Catherine spoke up first, saying, "I think at this point I need a few minutes to consult with my client. Could we have the room?" Tom agreed and suggested that he and both the constables leave the room.

Outside the interview room, George and Rabi were keen to ask again about planting trees, "sir what is it all about? we don't get it; what does planting a tree have to do with this interview?" "All will become very clear soon; I can tell you that the very fact we have been asked to leave the room for a few minutes means we have the upper hand here, and my question is working."

It wasn't long before Catherine appeared out of the room and asked Tom to return. They all entered the room again, taking up their original positions; Catherine spoke and said, "I do not know what trees have to do with all of this. However, it would appear to my client and me that the person you want the most is lord Vincent; if we agree to help you get a conviction, then what can we have in return?" Tom smiled to himself; his plan had worked; they are now asking for a deal, which means Bob knows more than he is letting on. "Well, Bob, it may be possible to arrange something, but I have to tell you, we know you moved the girls' bodies and made it look like one of my old cases from years ago. We both worked on that case together, that truly is unforgivable, not just in my eyes but with everyone. Having said all of this, Bob, I am sure we can sort something out, but first, would you please tell everyone when the best time to plant a tree is?" Bob looked at Catherine; she nodded her head in approval, and Bob began to speak, "The best time to plant a tree was twenty years ago; the second-best time to plant one is today." Suddenly everything made sense. George and Rabi understood what Tom was doing; he was reminding Bob that whatever had happened could not be changed, that time had passed. However, he could plant a new tree today by compensating for his mistakes, but it has to be today.

Tom told Catherine and Bob that if he cooperates and gives us the evidence needed to gain a conviction. Catherine replied, "ok, in exchange for our evidence and complete cooperation, we want a significant reduction in the sentence."

He was sure that he could get a significantly reduced sentence for his part in the crimes.

Tom replied, "of course, only if it directly leads to the conviction of lord Vincent." They all agreed, so Tom sat silently as Bob began his evidence against lord Vincent and explained his part. The interview continued for a few hours before Catherine stopped Bob and requested a break. Tom saw this as his opportunity to go and speak to the chief and ask for an arrest warrant for Lord Vincent.

"Great work Tom; I knew you could do it; just one question, what was all this I have heard about planting trees?" "It is a long story, sir; I will include it in my report for you if you like; for now, though, we need to go to Lord Vincent's house and arrest him for his part in all of this. Can we catch up in a while, sir?"

"Yes, Tom, but be careful there is no telling what a man like him may do when cornered!"

"Don't worry, sir, I never take chances.

Tom arranged three police cars and an unmarked car for himself. He had decided to drive, leading the way to the house of lord Vincent. He drove directly to the front door at speed. Although the house was undoubtedly impressive, it was nothing like his father-in-law's house. Tom calmly walked up to the front door and rang the bell. There was no answer; he was sure Vincent was in, he signalled to two of the other officers to stand at the front door whilst he took the others around the back.

He had not quite arrived at the patio doors that led into the orangery before he heard what sounded like a gunshot. Tom knew immediately what might have happened. He let himself in with two other officers following him, fully expecting to see Jane on the floor with lord Vincent standing over her with a gun.

To his surprise, he found Vincent lying across his desk with a pistol in his hand. It was clear to everyone that Vincent had committed suicide; on the floor, partially spattered with blood, was a letter addressed to Jane.

Tom knew the case was now over; he left the scene precisely as he found it and requested that a police photographer take pictures first for evidence. This is not how it was supposed to be, he thought to himself; he knew, of course, that he could not let on to Bob at this stage as he still needed all the information first. It was then that it dawned on him; he had told Jane about his plans over breakfast. Could Jane have put two and two together and realised what would happen? How did Vincent realise he was coming? Did Jane warn him of my plan, he thought. This was all Tom could think about as he made his way back to see the chief.

When he arrived, the custody sergeant met him at the back doors, "Sir, I have something to tell you, and it's not good I'm afraid, but you do need to know."

Tom was not in the mood to hear more bad news and almost dismissed him; however, the sergeant insisted more forcefully. "Sir, you need to know this; it is about Bob. I allowed him his one phone call. I assumed it would have been to his solicitor, but it wasn't, it was to lord Vincent, and he sent Catherine McEwen as his brief; Bob did not ask for one. Tom was not sure whether to be happy or angry at this stupid mistake, but at least he knew that Jane had not intervened in his case, knowing her husband would take the easy way out.

Tom briefed the chief on all the events, including how Bob had used his rightful phone call to tip off Vincent instead of calling a solicitor. The mood was sour, and the chief demanded that whatever happens now, there would be no deal for Bob, "he can rot in prison for all I care now. Whatever you have on him, Tom, make it stick, make it stick good. Tom agreed to do his best, left the room and headed back to the cells, "I want Bob in an interview room NOW! I don't care what his solicitor says, Rabi, George, with me." The look on Tom's face was virement; Tom was not taking any rubbish now.

Bob and his solicitor entered the room; Tom sat down as before and incredibly looked calm. "Ok, Bob, we have had a small break; let's get everything down on paper; the sooner we get this done, the better, wouldn't you say? Bob and Catherine agreed, not knowing what would happen next. after another two hours of talking, Bob had incriminated Vincent, himself and James into the whole mess. He told how the Girl's deaths were indeed a tragic accident, the drugs they had taken were too pure, and they should have been cut first. He also said how he had gotten these drugs for James from evidence, not knowing how pure they were.

"It should never have happened, you must understand it was a mistake!"

Tom looked at Bob and replied, "a mistake that cost two innocent girls their lives." Bob broke down crying; it took several minutes before they could carry on the interview.

Eventually, Bob said in his defence, "I only wanted out of fraud and back to London, lord Vincent promised me he could make this happen, he told me I was a good man, the sort they needed in his club."

Tom took no pleasure in what he was about to do. "Robert Jenkins, I am re-arresting you on further crimes to be added to the original charge sheet. There can be no deal owing to your actions earlier today. You deliberately and intentionally passed on information to lord Vincent with the express intention to pervert the course of justice and to help him evade arrest. I now have the unpleasant misfortune of informing his wife, Lady Jane Vincent, of her husband's suicide, and that is directly on you!"

Bob looked up directly towards Tom, his eyes bloodshot and almost relieved it was now all over, "I'm sorry Tom, I never wanted this to happen this way, it just all got out of my control."

Tom could only stand there listening to what Bob had to say. "I do have one more question for you, Bob; why make the two girls' deaths look like murder and our old case?

"That was a mistake on my part; I'd hoped that if I made it look like that old case, the chief, knowing I had been involved in it might then ask me for help. My plan was to then prove it was not murder but death by misadventure from drugs. Hopefully, the chief would be pleased and take me off fraud and put me on murder cases or suspicious deaths, perhaps even on drug cases. I didn't plan on them bringing you here. When I heard that you were on your way, I knew deep down that I had made a terrible mistake and that in truth it was now, all over. I am so sorry Tom, please forgive me for doing that to you?"

Tom never said a word; he stood and calmly left the room and headed to the chief's office to update him and officially ask him if he could now go home.

Chapter Thirty

Three weeks later

"Sir you asked to see me!" Tom asked in a chirpy manner.

"Yes, Tom. I've had a request."

Tom had been home almost three weeks when his boss, chief constable Genders, asked to see him. Instinct told Tom his perfect day was about to come to an end.

"What's the request, Sir?" The tone of Tom's voice was now lower and less happy.

"I have been handed a new case to be assigned to you personally."

"Sir, you know I only have two weeks left before I retire, What's the case? And why me?"

The look on Derek Gender's face already told a story of reluctance as he began to tell Tom about his new assignment.

"This morning," Derek sighed, "a little girl was reported missing; she had vanished from her house, leaving her two older brothers and mum asleep in bed."

"That's dreadful, sir; of course, I'll help but why me?"

"That's the question I'm asking myself. Of course, I told the home office you retire in two weeks, but they are insistent it has to be you."

"The home office. Since when do they get involved in these cases, and that still doesn't answer my question, why me!"

"You're right, Tom, but that is their request. They also said I should tell you it's an order and not a request if you refuse."

"So I don't have a choice then?"

"It would seem not, Tom. I'm sorry, but there it is. Either you have upset someone powerful, or that influential person likes you and only trusts you to do what's necessary.

Tom's emotions were torn; he felt compelled to help, but he promised Mary. He knew his retirement was essential to his family and him.

"Sir, I do have a holiday booked and not only that my daughter is due to come home from the hospital in the next few days. What am I going to do?"

"Tom, I don't know what to say! these are mine and your orders, although, I am sure with your skill and expertise you could solve this within the time you have left."

"But what if I can't? Will my replacement take over to allow me to retire?"

"I'm sorry Tom, you're replacement doesn't arrive for another three weeks. You're just going to have to do what you do best."

For the love of murder: The girl in the woods.

T om's story doesn't end here.
The girl in the woods is the second instalment in this new book series. (**For the love of murder**) It follows the story of a little girl determined to find her older sister only to discover a gruesome truth about humanity.

Tom only has a short while before he retires and may have to hand the case over to another detective.

Can he find the girl?

Who at the home office wants him on the case and why?

The story continues for Tom and us.

Acknowledgments

So my story is finally finished, or is it?

Writing this book has not so much been about the challenge of doing so. However, being honest, it has had its challenges, as I am sure many writers, including those that would be, will tell you. It has, however, been a journey; I started it just before my wife was diagnosed with Breast cancer, and our daughter was at the tender age of fourteen. This book represents the period when I chose my family over anything else in my life, including my career. The journey became about looking after my wife and daughter, helping them both come to terms with what was happening. This investment in us as a family paid off in ways we could never imagine. In the eight years that passed, we nursed my wife back to excellent health, home-schooled our daughter, downsized our home and moved to Southern Ireland from Essex. We made new friends, experienced different cultures, and learned to appreciate life in a way we could never dream of.

In recent weeks, I decided to return to writing after such a significant gap in a bid to write something for my wife of 27 years and best friend to enjoy. However, the cancer is back and is now life-limiting.

We are all in a more robust place, sure we know there are joyous days. Some that are less so; however, together, we started this journey and together, we will see it through. I am so proud to say we are a family that can laugh together and, on occasion, also cry together.

I love you very much.

I believe that apart from acknowledging my family's support, for which I will always be eternally grateful. I must also recognise some unsung heroes in our lives.

First of all, our close friends, I will not embarrass you by adding your names. You know who you are even if you would prefer not to admit that in public.

The charity, **Carers First** (Carrie-Anne) have been a great support, a listening ear and on occasion delivered cream teas and chocolate to our home. Secondly, some excellent organisations starting with the **Radiotherapy unit in Colchester**, the doctors and nurses of **Broomfield hospital Chelmsford,** all of whom work tirelessly for everyone's benefit, especially during Covid. Then, of course, the ladies who support us all from the **Mcmillan booth also at Broomfield hospital** (Thank you for the listening ear, the tissues and support.) Again, a big thank you to my favourite **international coffee lady at Broomfield hospital.**

There is one more huge thank you which must go out to a special lady who, through her adversity in life, turned her experience into a way to help others. "Jane" from a fantastic organisation called **Peabody's**, your support made a difference in our lives. Thank you, everyone; you are the stars that shine in the darkened skies.

Printed in Great Britain
by Amazon

17953751R00123